Perdition's
Child

Perdition's Child

Book 4 in the Hannah Weybridge series

Anne Coates

Urbane
PUBLICATIONS

urbanepublications.com

First published in Great Britain in 2020 by Urbane Publications Ltd
Unit E3 The Premier Centre Abbey Park Romsey SO51 9DG
Copyright © Anne Coates, 2020

A CIP catalogue record for this book is available from the British Library.

ISBN 978-1-912666-67-6
MOBI 978-1-912666-68-3

Design and Typeset by Julie Martin
Cover by Julie Martin

Printed and bound by 4edge UK

urbanepublications.com

For everyone who has ever lost a child.

"Excellent wretch, perdition catch my soul
But I do love thee, and when I love thee not,
Chaos is come again."

Othello, Shakespeare

"And none of them is lost but the son of perdition."

St John's Gospel 17:12

CHAPTER ONE
Monday 27 June, 1994

The stairwell echoed with the ungainly clump of her footsteps. Her weathered walking boots with unmatched knotted and frayed laces were far too hot and heavy for summer – even with the flow of air offered through various holes – and these last few weeks had been sweltering. Her feet were hot and clammy; a blister had formed where the back rubbed her heel. Whenever she removed her socks layers of skin flaked away. Her feet, more than any other part of her body, disgusted her. Between her toes were signs of an infection. She'd tried talking to the chemist in Boots down The Marsh, but he wanted to see her feet. Her embarrassment overcame her discomfort, so she left without showing him. But these boots were the only footwear she possessed. Flip Flops she thought. Or those plastic sandals. What were they called? Jellies. Silly name. They were cheap. She should store these bloody boots somewhere; or better still get rid of them so her feet could heal in the sun and air.

Her clothes, which had long since lost any of their original colour and shape, stuck to some parts of her body and hung from others. Beneath her skirt, the flesh at the top of her thighs was rubbed raw. There were times when she wished she could peel off her skin and start again. In the depths of night when no one could see her, she wept. Tears were sometimes the only liquid to touch her face for days on end. A caress no person would give.

She paused at the second landing, breathing heavily. The smells of leftover food wafted over from the waste disposal chute with its ornate black front, which never completely closed on what had been thrown into it. Lucy wondered if anyone ever cleaned it. Her mother used to. Not here, but in the similar block of 1930s flats they had lived in nearby. Her mother had scrubbed the steps as well. The steps she used to run up two at a time in her eagerness to get home. How long ago was that? Too long ago to think about. A lifetime ago.

On the third floor she rested against the wall, rubbing her hand, sticky from the balustrade, on her skirt. One more bit of dirt wouldn't show. She stared out over the sun-dappled square. Everywhere looked so much better in the sunshine. Strangely, there was no one around. No kids on skateboards. No dealers loitering in the shadows. No one screaming obscenities from an open window. An enormous ginger cat, balancing precariously on a window ledge, stared at her disdainfully for a moment then carried on with his meticulous grooming. Everywhere seemed still and quiet. Unnaturally so. Maybe the heat had sucked out the energy from the residents.

She continued her climb, gripping the rail. Panting she reached the fourth floor and wiped her sleeve across her brow. The fabric was stiff with sweat and snot and heaven knows what else. God, she needed a wash. She remembered the public baths in Wells Street. A luxury now closed. She shook the memory away as she hobbled along the walkway to number 39 and banged loudly on the door. Harry was going deaf but claimed he heard her footsteps coming even when he couldn't hear the knocking on the door. Not that they seemed to have alerted him this time.

She knocked again, more loudly. The tiny scullery window was open behind the bars that protected it. That meant he must be in. He always shut that window when he went out even though a kitten would struggle to gain access through it. Nothing. She bent forward and shouted through the letterbox.

"Harry! Harry! Can you hear me? It's me. Lucy." There was no reply.

She peered through the letterbox. The sitting room was in darkness, the door ajar, but there was a light on in the hallway. That was strange. Harry was never one to burn the electric unnecessarily. Tight sod. She stood up, supporting her back with her hand as she did so, and wondered what to do. Harry was always in at this time of the day. Not that she visited him very often. Only as a last resort. He rarely went out now. Or so he told her. She heard he still managed to get to the pub. Perhaps he had just popped out for something and she should wait.

A door opened along the walkway. A woman with short purple hair, barefooted and wearing a long loose green floral skirt which clashed with her red and blue striped t-shirt, came out and lit a cigarette. "All right?"

"Not sure." She found talking with strangers difficult. Awkward. Words seemed to cling to her tongue. "Harry – have you seen him going out?"

"Saw him last week. Think it was Tuesday when he goes to collect his pension. But I've been away for a few days."

Lucy considered the woman and wondered how much

she knew of Harry's comings and goings. Today was Monday.

"Well 'e's not 'ere now." She scratched the place where her hair was pulled back with an old tie she'd found near a school at end of the summer term last year. "I'll come back later. I'm 'is sister."

The woman stubbed out her cigarette in an ashtray on the windowsill and stared at Lucy but not unpleasantly. "I know who you are." She turned to go back into her flat. "Wait there a moment. I've got his spare key."

Lucy wondered whether she should let herself in. What if Harry came back to find her and the neighbour inside his flat? He was a suspicious and secretive man. On the other hand, he could have been taken ill. Or maybe he had fallen?

The woman returned and unlocked the door, then stood aside for Lucy to enter before following her in. The overwhelming stench of decaying flesh combined with the low murmur of bluebottles made the neighbour heave and she ran out of the flat, calling, "I'll phone the police."

Lucy's less refined sensibilities coped a little longer as she rushed across the sitting room and opened the curtains and a window.

Harry – or what was left of him – was sitting in his usual armchair, facing the three TV sets he had balanced on top of each other. He liked to have all three switched on at once so, he said, he would miss nothing on any of the channels. A job working for the civil service before an early retirement had given him an inflated sense of his own importance. Especially when he received the

British Empire Medal, and the letter had been signed by 'Your obedient servant', something he never missed an opportunity to mention.

In the afternoon light that filtered through grubby windows, his body was bloated, grotesque. The ashtray was full, one cigarette reduced to a long line of ash. A glass was on the table beside him, half-filled with his usual tipple, Guinness. Now with a layer of gunge on top instead of the iconic froth. Lucy stared. An avalanche of emotions competed with each other. Suddenly the bile rose and she dashed to the bathroom just in time to spew the contents of her stomach.

When she emerged, the neighbour took her by the wrist, led her outside and shut the door. "The police will be here soon. Sit here. Lucy isn't it?" She'd brought a kitchen chair out onto the walkway. Bright yellow plastic. Easily cleaned. "I'm Edith."

Lucy nodded. "Thanks." The woman moved away from her. She stank. She knew that. But at least it was the healthy smell of a live person. She felt her stomach clench again. Edith gently guided a glass of water into her hand. "Would you like a cup of tea?" Her offer was almost drowned by the sound of a police siren, which stopped abruptly as the car came into the forecourt, shortly followed by an ambulance they'd have no need for.

Wiping her mouth with the back of her hand, Lucy braced herself for questions she either didn't want to respond to or ones she didn't know the answer to. Harry had a lot to answer for, but he hadn't deserved an end like this.

At the police station, in a small, bleak, grey interview room and a tiny, square window (which offered little natural light), Lucy sat opposite a woman in uniform and a plain-clothes officer who had introduced himself as DS Benton. There was a vague familiarity about him, but she wasn't sure why. She didn't trust his smile and she noticed that he sat back in his chair, hands thrust in his trouser pockets, as though to put as much distance as he could between himself and her stench. As though poverty and all the indignities that went with it were contagious.

"Lucy is there anyone who could be here with you?" Benton asked. "Maybe the woman who lived next door to your brother?"

"Why? You don't think I 'ad anything to do with him dying do you? Anyway I don't know her."

He looked concerned but avoided answering the question. "It would be better for you to have a friend or someone else with you. It must have been a terrible shock to find your brother like that."

It was. She could still taste the bile even after two cups of strong, sweet tea. For a moment her mind went blank. Who did she know? Who could she ask to come here? Who was even contactable? No one in the Bull Ring. She had no one. Then the fog in her brain cleared. There was someone.

"Ask Hannah. Hannah Weybridge." She added the surname for good measure.

Benton coughed to cover the expletive he'd just uttered. "I'm sorry?"

Lucy ignored him. "Wait a moment, I've got her

number somewhere." She rummaged in her bag and fished out a card, now grubby and bent.

"Would you like me to phone her for you?" asked the woman officer who had introduced herself as Sheridan James. She had a gentle Welsh accent and a kind smile.

Lucy nodded. She wouldn't have trusted herself to make the call. The female officer took the card and touched her lightly on the shoulder before she went out of the room, leaving the door open. Lucy rocked on her seat. If anyone could help her, she thought, Hannah could and would. At least she hoped so. Although she still wasn't quite sure why she needed help.

Benton opened a packet of cigarettes and handed her one. She took it gratefully. "How d'you know Ms Weybridge then?"

Lucy eyed him through a smoke circle she'd just exhaled. "Her friend Liz Rayman who got murdered in St John's church." She stated the fact as though it explained everything. Benton wanted to ask more but Sheridan returned.

"Sorry Lucy. Hannah's away. On holiday. She's not due back for a couple of days, according to her mother. Is there anyone else?"

Lucy blew another smoke ring. "Yeah. I suppose so." She made another foray into the recesses of her bag and this time pulled out a slightly cleaner business card.

Benton nearly choked on his cigarette as he inspected the embossed lettering: Simon Ryan QC. How in God's name did she have his card?

Sheridan gave the detective a withering glance. "I'll see if I can get through to him."

Lucy and Benton smoked on in the uneasy quiet she left behind her.

"How d'you come to be so pally with Simon Ryan then?" Benton broke the silence after offering Lucy a second cigarette.

"I'm not pally with him." Lucy inhaled deeply and glared at Benton. "His brother, Father Patrick, was murdered," she said, as if that told him everything he needed to know.

"And now your brother's dead." The words were out before he could stop himself. He hadn't meant to sound so unsympathetic.

Lucy stared at him. "But Harry wasn't murdered, was he." It wasn't a question. She assumed Harry had had a heart attack or something. She was about to say something more when the female officer came back into the room.

"Well you certainly have friends in high places, Lucy. Mr Ryan is contacting a London solicitor who should be here within the hour. In the meantime, he suggested we take you for some lunch. Would the canteen here be okay for you?"

Benton muttered something under his breath, which Lucy couldn't make out, but she caught the gist of it from his expression. If she hadn't felt so sick from the sight of her brother, she might have enjoyed his discomfort. But a free lunch wasn't to be sneezed at whatever the circumstances.

CHAPTER TWO

Elizabeth was calling, her chubby arms outstretched. "Mama…" her rosebud lips transformed the word into a smile, as she ran towards her… The shot rang out. Hannah sat bolt upright in bed, her heart pounding against her ribcage, her breathing choking her. It took her a moment or two to realise where she was. To adjust her brain to the here and now. She was alone in the hotel room but could see Tom standing out on the balcony beyond the almost transparent curtain, which was moving in the gentlest of breezes. As the adrenaline rush subsided, she tied a sarong around herself, and joined him.

He slipped an arm around her shoulders, giving her a comforting squeeze. "Just a car backfiring." He smiled reassuringly, but all Hannah could see were the dark circles under his eyes. His haunted expression. His hurt.

"You didn't sleep well again."

She turned to face him, and he pulled her close. "No," he said into her hair so that the word was barely more than a breath. "Sorry if I disturbed you."

Hannah had learned more from his nighttime exclamations than anything he had told her about being in the New York café when it was blown up, killing and injuring over fifty people. "When we get back you need to follow through with the psychologist you were offered."

After Tom had returned and they both survived the assassination attempt at the RAF Northolt, they had attended the reception hosted by Lord Gyles, the proprietor of *The News*. The story was front-page news and the newspaper had paid for Hannah and Tom to stay in a suite at the Savoy for a few days until the interest died down. Janet brought Elizabeth to join them, and, cocooned in luxury, they were able to discuss some of what had happened while Tom was in New York. It was a bittersweet time. Hannah had her own nightmares to contend with, but Tom's experiences had left him with both physical and mental wounds, which were profoundly disturbing.

After those few days, which seemed like a hiatus in time, Tom was taken off for debriefing and Hannah returned home. A visit to Corfu had been a chance for them to unwind together, but if anything Tom's demons seemed to have more of a hold on him. Now they were at the end of their holiday.

"I know." He took her hand and brushed it lightly with his thumb. "That's something else we need to talk about."

"What?" Hannah thought she knew what was coming. It had been hovering between them all the time they had been together. No amount of sun, sea and sex could obliterate the pain and trauma Tom had been through. His physical wounds sustained in New York were healing well. The scars a reminder but not a traumatic one. What he had gone through mentally was a different matter. Hannah wondered what the US authorities had exposed him to. Although he tried to disguise his anguish, during the night Hannah was often woken by his disturbed thoughts breaking through the nightmares. It had been a trying time for both of them.

"I don't think I can make any commitments to you – and Elizabeth – while I am like this …" Hannah opened her mouth to say something. "No, let me finish, please. This is hard enough. You must know how I feel about you. But right now, I'm all over the place. This holiday has been wonderful in so many ways, but it's also made me realise any attempt at life as a couple, a family, is beyond me at the moment."

Hannah hugged him tightly. She felt guilty at the tiny glimmer of relief she felt. Her joy at discovering Tom had survived the bombing outrage in New York was tempered by the changes in him. They both had their demons, but Tom's were more vociferous. In her own vulnerable state, she felt unequal to helping him.

Side-by-side they stood looking out to the sea and beach that had been their view for a week. Time on their own as Hannah's parents had come over from France to be with Elizabeth, while Janet maintained her usual routine during the daytime. Hannah had been dubious about leaving her daughter but in retrospect it was the right thing to do. A toddler wouldn't have understood Tom's outbursts. His grief. His rage. His silences. His torment. Sometimes she wasn't sure she could either.

Hannah had felt the healing effects of the sun and relaxation. She was saddened they hadn't worked in any measure on Tom but her time with the counsellor she had seen after Liz's death and the attempt to kill Elizabeth had had long-term beneficial effects. She had learned, to a certain extent, how to control bad thoughts and …

"I'm going to be away for a while." Tom's voice broke into her thoughts. "It's a sort of rehab clinic."

Hannah was taken aback. "And how long have you known about this?"

Tom stared out to sea. "It was arranged before we left. I had hoped – oh I don't know, that maybe being away together would effect some miracle cure."

His smile tore her apart. She wanted desperately to be his cure but she knew deep down he needed more and she had Elizabeth to care for.

As she had left the hotel, Hannah glanced at the man in the lobby who had accompanied them. Throughout their stay – except when they were safely ensconced in their room – he was never more than a metre or so away from Tom. She was amused at the variety of guises he had used in the hope of blending in. Sometimes she saw him approach Tom and say something, which she never could hear. Lip-reading, she thought, would be a useful skill to acquire. It was clear who his priority was. He never followed her. Hannah didn't know whether she felt relieved or miffed. At least she didn't seem to be a target any more. But it horrified her that the powers that be thought Tom still could be. From what he had told her, the little he had been allowed to reveal, some members of the syndicate in the US, which was part of the global ring trafficking young girls, were protected from the judiciary. Probably some were part of the government forces expected to protect their citizens. It made Hannah feel hollow inside. Corruption at the core of society. At least here they could forget for a while.

The holiday had been arranged and paid for by Lord Gyles who had seen his newspaper's ratings rise dramatically with the exclusive coverage it had received. Not for the first time Hannah wondered about Lord Gyles' links to government and or the secret services. He had suggested a longer break but Hannah couldn't bear the thought of being separated from Elizabeth for more than a week.

Dipping her feet in the sea and letting the ripples of sand ebb and flow between her toes, Hannah gazed along the beach and thought it would be a wonderful place to bring Elizabeth. They hadn't had a proper holiday together yet. A bucket and spade holiday. She needed to start building up the happy memories for them to cherish in years to come. She thought of their brief trip to Brighton with Tom. That seemed a lifetime ago. Why did bad memories stretch out and haunt you while good ones were over in the blink of an eye?

"A drachma for them?"

Hannah looked up shading her eyes. "Not sure about the exchange rate."

Tom carefully manouevered himself down beside her on the sand. His right leg was still stiff from the metal plates that had been screwed onto his bones to help repair his injuries. He rarely mentioned the pain. But Hannah could see the concerted effort in his expression. "Might be able to manage two?"

In her peripheral vision, Hannah saw the protection officer lowering himself into a deckchair and opening a book. Hannah noticed it was always the same book he seemed to be in the middle of and smiled knowing that behind the reflective sunglasses his eyes would be scanning the environment, not the type on the page. "I was thinking of another beach – Brighton. How Elizabeth had loved paddling and the waves. I should bring her here."

"Good idea." He stared out at a small boat moving across the horizon. He remembered their weekend in Brighton. When he was a different man. "I am so sorry."

"What for?"

"Everything I've put you through."

Hannah laughed but there was a bitterness in her voice. "Join the queue – I don't think you're my number one culprit."

He had the sense not to ask her who that was. For a moment they were silent. Each thinking they probably knew the other's thoughts. Each wondering how they would hold it together before parting yet again.

"While I am away, I –" Tom took her hand and stared at her palm as though seeing the future. "I won't be contactable for a while. I have to go through – well I'm not sure what I'll be going through. But I will give you a number where you can leave a message if you need help in any way." His thumb stroked her fingers. "Sorry, it's the best I can offer for the time being."

Hannah leaned her body against his and absorbed the warmth. There was nothing she could say. But she wanted to reassure him. No reassure was the wrong word. Release might be better. She didn't want his progress to be hampered by worries about her. It took every ounce of her self-control to say, "Put yourself first. Don't worry about me or what might or might not happen in the future. No pressure."

She smiled and gently touched the face she'd grown to

love but now had to let go. "But you must contact me if ... if ... well when you can or want to." She took a deep breath and looked at her watch, stood up and offered her hand. "Come on, it's time to check out."

As they stood facing each other, their bodies so nearly touching, Hannah thought her heart, or at least a part of it, would break.

Corfu Airport, Ioannis Kapodistrias, was not far away and the three of them sat in the taxi silently, each with their own thoughts, the protection officer in the front passenger seat. Tom clasped Hannah's hand tightly. He stared straight ahead, his expression unreadable. Inside Hannah was screaming. Life was so unfair. Just when she thought she had got him back, Tom was being taken from her again.

They arrived at the airport. Another goodbye. They weren't even flying back together as they were, she had discovered, heading for different UK destinations. The protection officer wished her a safe journey and both men walked to the departure gate, neither looking back.

CHAPTER THREE

DS Benton was sitting at his desk, a file open in front of him. But he wasn't reading. He was thinking about his interview with Lucy Peters and how Hannah Weybridge's name had come up. The two women were only tenuously linked by the deaths of Hannah's friend and the vicar of St John's but Lucy felt she could call on her. Interesting – the bag lady and the journalist. Try as he might he couldn't reconcile all the facts he knew about Hannah. He had grown to admire her in an offhand sort of way and he knew the DI and she had grown quite friendly. As far as anyone could be friendly with the Ice Queen. What made that woman tick? She gave nothing away of her personal life and as far as he knew there was no Mr Turner on the scene. Or even a Ms Turner. He wondered not for the first time about her friendship with Tom Jordan. Now what had become of him? He'd disappeared again. Life can't be easy after what he'd been through. Poor sod.

His phone buzzed and one of the subjects of his musings asked him to pop into her office. DI Claudia Turner smiled as he entered.

"Have a seat Mike." She opened her desk drawer and produced a bottle and two glasses. "Not too early – ?"

Mike shook his head. "Are we celebrating something?"

"You tell me." Claudia would have made an excellent poker player.

Benton took a sip of his drink and placed his glass carefully on the desk.

"Are you blushing Sergeant?"

"No guv." His embarrassment was obvious.

"Okay." Claudia shuffled some papers in front of her then looked up, a huge grin on her face. "Congratulations on passing your inspector's exam. Though I hope you won't be leaving us too soon." She topped up their glasses. "We'll have a proper celebration when this Harry Peters case is wrapped up."

Benton grinned at her. It had been at the DI's suggestion that he took his inspector's exam. He had thought he wasn't in with a chance. But happily he'd been proved wrong.

"Thanks Guv." He raised his glass to her. "Have we got anything to go on with Harry Peters?"

"Just got the preliminary PM report." She passed it over to him.

"I thought that was a natural." He started reading. "Obviously I was mistaken." He took a large gulp of his drink.

"That fact goes no further." The DI looked concerned. "Apparently it's difficult to know if poison was administered as he had been dead so long. The pathologist is doing more tests..."

"Something was odd in that room."

"What the three TV sets balanced on top of each other?"

"Yes." Benton paused. "Apparently he watched them all at the same time, but they had been switched off."

"So?"

"So someone else had been there either before or after his death."

"It wasn't that the money had run out in his meter?"

"No, because the hall light was left on."

Claudia took a sip of her drink. "What did you make of his sister –" Turner flicked some papers – "Lucy?"

"She's not so daft as she looks."

"Meaning?"

"She had the nouse to keep the business cards of Hannah Weybridge and Simon Ryan QC. And used them to good effect when we interviewed her."

Claudia laughed and took another sip of whisky. "You need to get over that Mike. A homeless person having friends in high places, whatever next."

Mike contemplated his drink. "Still, I don't think she's a murderer. Let's face it, if she wanted to kill her brother she'd have done it years ago."

"Why? She might just have discovered something that he'd done in the past, or something he knew of and didn't tell her?"

"True." Benton wasn't convinced.

"And remember this is someone living all her life on her wits. It can't have been easy living rough all this time. With a brother living nearby."

"If she was."

"What d'you mean?" Claudia studied her sergeant's face. She appreciated that he had a different way of assessing the facts. They made a good team. Complementing each other. But for how much longer?

"Apparently she used to disappear for weeks sometimes months on end. No one knew where she went. Then she'd just reappear and carry on as before."

"No law against that, as far as I know. I wonder why her brother didn't help her, though?"

"Well I don't get on with my brother. I can't imagine him helping me out. Who can account for families?"

"Speaking of which you'd better go home to yours."

Mike finished his drink. At the door he paused. "Any news on Tom Jordan?"

Claudia looked thoughtful. "No he seems to have been whisked away somewhere. Rehab or so the story goes."

"And you don't believe that because…"

Claudia fiddled with a pen on her desk. "Something doesn't feel right. But maybe it's just my suspicious nature."

"Goes with the job."

"Yes but I wonder what Hannah makes of it?"

Mike drummed his fingers on the doorframe. "I wonder if Lucy has contacted her? Ms Weybridge keeps strange friends."

Claudia laughed. "Am I included in that category?"

Mike's demeanour was that of a schoolboy caught smoking behind the bike sheds.

"Go home, Mike. I'm teasing you."

A tease was the last description Benton would have applied to his boss. "Night Guv."

She smiled, knowing how much she was going to miss him when his promotion came through.

CHAPTER FOUR

The warm sunshine on her body was just the tonic Hannah needed to counteract her sadness as she walked up Barry Road to the library. Once she got there, she'd read all the national and local newspapers checking for stories that might just lead her to something more engaging than interviewing the 'UK's Most Romantic Couple' which was the latest job *The News* had assigned her.

She sensed rather than heard the person following her and paused at the bus stop, ostensibly to check something in her bag. The woman behind her carried on walking. Hannah's breathing deepened. Would there ever come a time when her instincts wouldn't go into overdrive she wondered. Maybe it was worrying about Tom and the fact that he'd had a protection officer on holiday with them that had sharpened her senses.

She was deep in memories of their time in Corfu as she rounded the top of the road so at first wasn't aware that the traffic was being diverted. There were two police cars outside the library. It was only after she'd crossed Lordship Lane she noticed the police tape across the main entrance.

A uniformed officer stood by the tape. "Sorry Miss, the library's closed – could be for the rest of the day."

"What's happened?" All this seemed rather dramatic outside the imposing, stately building, one of Hannah's favourites, that had stood there for nearly one hundred years on this corner. A library was hardly a den of iniquity.

The officer coughed as paramedics came out of the main doors carrying a stretcher. The black body bag was answer enough. Hannah wondered if the deceased was one of the regulars she saw in the upstairs reference room where all the day's papers and magazines were available.

She caught sight of a small group of people who were clustered around in the area leading to the garden. One woman was crying. She recognised the chief librarian she often chatted to, Natalie Vines. In her forties, Natalie was tall and slim with long dark hair and was always smartly dressed. Today she looked crumpled. From this distance Hannah couldn't make out her expression but the way she was standing suggested she was in shock. Hannah knew how she felt. She didn't think she would ever forget finding her friend's dead body in the crypt at St John's Waterloo. It was only six months ago but still felt like yesterday.

A police officer approached the group and looked as though he was taking down their details. Hannah hung back to see if Natalie would be leaving any time soon. She was in luck.

"Natalie!" The librarian walked over towards her. The police officer lifted the tape for her. She smiled her thanks.

"You look as though you could do with a drink."

"Hello Hannah." Natalie stood up straighter. "You're right. I could do with sitting down as well."

They crossed the road to The Plough. Hannah sometimes popped over to the pub for lunch when she was working in the library – and to use their loos in preference to the Portaloo outside the library.

It was early for the regulars so there were plenty of tables to choose from. Natalie moved towards a window seat.

"What can I get you? A brandy?"

Natalie nodded. "Thank you."

Hannah returned with some drinks. "Did you know the man who died?"

Natalie took a gulp of brandy then coughed. "He's been in nearly every day for the last week or so. He was the type of man you notice. Tall. Tanned. Australian accent. Easy smile." She took another sip of her drink and coughed again. Her hands were shaking as she placed her glass carefully on the table.

"Natalie you look dreadful. Would you like me to book you a cab home?"

"Not just yet. I need to tell you..."

"Oh here you are – we wondered where you'd disappeared to." Two assistant librarians Hannah knew by sight only joined them. It was obvious they were waiting to be offered a drink but neither Hannah nor Natalie obliged.

"Right shall we get ourselves a drink then?" one asked the other and they both went to the bar, their demeanour expressing their displeasure.

"Before they get back, here's my telephone number and address. There was something very strange about the death of that poor man."

Hannah picked up the slip of paper and handed Natalie her card. Strange deaths seemed to haunt her. "I'll get you a cab." She phoned the mini cab company she regularly used. "Right one's on its way." The two young women exchanged a glance as they joined them.

Natalie finished her drink. "Thanks. Bye you two. See you tomorrow. We should be open again then." Hannah followed her out and saw her into the cab she'd booked on her account.

"Is there someone at home, Natalie?" The librarian nodded. "Call me if you need to." Hannah shut the door and watched the car drive away, then went back into the pub.

"Can I get you another drink?" For a moment she thought they were going to refuse.

"We're both drinking bottled lager, thanks," the younger girl replied. Hannah returned with their drinks and an orange juice for herself.

"So who found the body?"

"He wasn't a body. He was alive – I found him slumped over one of the desks. I got Jill to call an ambulance. I didn't really know what to do. He wasn't bleeding or anything. Just this terrible colour and wheezing. He wasn't wearing a tie but I loosened his collar." She took a long gulp of her lager. "Then he keeled over onto the floor."

The other assistant found her voice. "The ambulance had just arrived but there was nothing they could do. The police cleared the library and that was that... We gave our names and addresses and they asked us what had happened."

"To be honest they didn't seem too bothered..."

"Really?" Hannah sipped her orange juice. "Not every day someone dies in a library, I would have thought."

She made a mental note to phone DI Turner to see what she may have heard.

CHAPTER FIVE

As Hannah walked back the way she'd come only an hour earlier, her mind went over the curious phone call she'd had from Lucy the day before inviting her to visit her. Cardboard City, it appeared, was no longer her home. She was staying at a flat in Drayton House, in Waterloo. Hannah was intrigued and had agreed to go there that afternoon. On the way back she bought some flowers to take with her.

Her mother had told her that while she was away a woman police officer had rung asking whether Hannah could sit in with someone being interviewed. Hannah was furious that she hadn't taken a note of the message – as Janet would have done. In fact Janet wouldn't have answered the phone. She'd have let it go through to the answerphone, which is what Hannah had asked her mother to do. But her mother couldn't stop herself. She had to interfere. Impose herself. Plus she hadn't taken down any of the details. When Hannah mentioned that, her mother's retort had been, "I'm not your secretary, you know." It was all Hannah could do not to let it escalate into a full-bloodied row.

When she had returned from her holiday with Tom, alone and tired from travelling, there was an icy atmosphere between her parents and Janet, which almost dampened the joy she felt at seeing Elizabeth. Old resentments between mother and daughter resurfaced. Hannah had given Janet the gift she'd bought her and offered her the following day off. "You can enjoy a long weekend. They'll be gone when you return," she whispered. Janet smiled but said nothing.

Her mother couldn't wait to question her as soon as Janet had left. "So what's happening between you and Tom, then?"

Hannah could feel all the familiar animosity well up. Her mother's attitude was guaranteed to rile her. No sensitivity to her feelings. No sense of boundaries. Then she looked at her mother's face. Properly. She saw the worry lines. The sadness. The fear. And beyond that she saw the love. The love her mother found almost impossible to express.

She hugged her mother tightly. "To be honest, Mum, I just don't know."

Her mother moved away. Too much contact for her liking. "So where is he now?"

Hannah sighed. Her mother wouldn't take the hint. "In a rehabilitation centre. And I don't know where it is, before you ask."

Her mother gave her one of her "looks" but wisely changed the subject.

Hannah's father had obviously taken his role as grandfather seriously and was sitting on the floor with Elizabeth, happily helping her create some complicated building with her wooden bricks. Her daughter managed to make her mother smile as well and the rest of the day passed smoothly enough.

Hannah caught up with her post and emails. That evening her mother produced her signature coque au vin which was accompanied with plenty of wine and some reminiscences.

"I was sorry to hear about Paul." Her mother embraced another topic of conversation Hannah would rather have avoided. "It must have been a very difficult time for you."

"Yes it was." Hannah knew she had to be circumspect. What had appeared in the newspaper was far from the whole story.

"A dreadful thing for Elizabeth to find out when she's older." Daphne was on a roll of righteous indignation.

"Mum he may have acted unwisely but he wasn't to blame for..."

"Exposing you and his daughter to physical danger?" Two bright spots of red had appeared on her mother's cheeks. Maybe she'd had too much wine.

"But he didn't. He saved Elizabeth and Janet."

At the mention of the nanny's name, her mother pursed her lips. "Are you sure she wasn't in on it?"

"Oh for God's sake!" Hannah's anger made her skin burn.

Her mother was not to be deflected. "Don't say I didn't warn you." She realised she had gone too far when Hannah made to leave the table.

"I think she's a very pleasant young woman and she obviously thinks the world of Elizabeth."

Hannah smiled at her father. "She does and I'm very lucky to have her. And if it wasn't for the money I earn at *The News* I wouldn't be able to employ her. So that should answer the other question you are about to ask. Yes I still have my contract with them."

Hannah's mother looked as though she was going to

say something more but her husband caught her eye and shook his head.

"Your mother and I are proud of the stories you've covered. Personally I never thought you had it in you." Hannah felt another arrow of disappointment. Her father's approval had meant so much to her and here he was diminishing his praise with a lack of confidence in her skills. He finished the wine in his glass. "But dear God please be careful." He seemed dangerously close to tears.

Hannah covered his hand with her own. "I will, I promise. Now who's for cheese?"

The next morning, her parents were up early, packed and ready to leave. Her father was having a last play with Elizabeth. Hannah loved hearing them chatting away to each other. She wondered if he had played with her that way. Probably not. He'd have been working all hours.

Her mother was fussing with her bag. "I've only your best interests as heart, you know."

"I know. But that doesn't explain why you had to sell up and move to France." Hannah hadn't intended to say that although it was always uppermost in her mind when she thought of her parents.

Her mother chose to ignore that comment. "I'll tell your father I'm ready to leave."

"Mum…"

Hannah almost said, "Don't go. Don't leave me," but the thought did not translate into words. "Thanks. Thank you for being here."

Her mother smiled. "Have to get to see my

granddaughter somehow. Come over and stay with us soon, won't you?"

Hannah promised she would but there was a part of her that still resented what she saw as her mother's desertion when they moved to France just after she'd told them she was pregnant.

Her parents left for their home in the Loire and on Monday Janet was back. That was over a week ago and life had returned to the precarious sort of normal she had come to expect. She had had no word from Tom but consoled herself with the thought that that was probably a good sign.

Hannah picked her way carefully up the litter-strewn stairwell of Drayton House, checking where she trod as she climbed the stairs to the fourth floor, as Lucy had directed. The smells of cooking and refuse, made more unsavoury in the heat, mingled unappetisingly making her feel slightly nauseous. Some attempt had been made to tone down the graffiti that decorated the walls. A faded *George Davis is innocent* competed with football teams and some surprisingly good artwork of a cricket match. Each floor resembled the last with subtle differences. A young woman with Titian red hair streaked with purple manouevered a buggy past her coming down. Hannah smiled. "Can I give you a hand?"

The young woman laughed. "Nah yer alright I'm well used to it now." As an afterthought she added, "Thanks anyway," and carried on her way.

Reaching the fourth floor, Hannah paused on the walkway and viewed the square made by the buildings, criss-crossed with washing lines bearing the history, the present and perhaps the future of the people who lived here. Then she knocked at number 39.

"Well you're a sight for sore eyes," Lucy greeted her. "Come in. Come in." She all but pulled her into the dark, narrow hall then led her into the sitting room. "You've put on some weight." Lucy looked her up and down. "Suits you." Hannah wasn't sure how to reply and handed her the flowers. "Thanks I love roses." She buried her face in the bouquet. "Don't think anyone's ever given me flowers before." She left the room abruptly. Hannah heard noises from the scullery and Lucy returned with the roses in a vase, which she carefully placed on the sideboard.

"Bet you're surprised to see me 'ere," she said turning to Hannah, her face flushed. Hannah hadn't seen her since May at the interment of Father Patrick's ashes at Southwark Cathedral. She had sat with her and Beano in The George afterwards and had been intrigued by Lucy's concern and empathy for Simon Ryan when he joined them

"I'm not sure anything would surprise me about you Lucy, you're such an enterprising woman." Hannah smiled but she didn't know how wrong she was.

"My brother lived here. After our mam died he had to give up the two-bed flat they lived in and was moved to this one."

Hannah wondered why Lucy had not lived with them but didn't like to ask. Lucy would tell her what she wanted her to know. "He died. 'Suspicious death' they reckon. I was questioned at the police station and a nice young policewoman rang you for me. But you were away." Lucy's words sounded like an accusation but that did explain the call her mother had mentioned. "They said I needed someone with me so then I asked them to phone Father Patrick's brother and he got someone to come and sort things."

"That was good of him." Hannah was bemused that an eminent QC would sort out a minor problem for a homeless woman. Maybe he shared his brother's Christian values.

"He'd been dead for over a week," Lucy's words broke into her thoughts. "Found him sitting in his armchair, a half empty glass of Guinness on the table beside him.

"Thought he was just drunk at first but the smell ... well as you can imagine me nose has learned not to be too sensitive but Jesus it was awful. The neighbour who had a key and let me in called the police."

Lucy poured some of her tea into the saucer and blew on it. She'd made Hannah a coffee and they were sitting in the room that presumably the brother had died in. It was a square room with one tall, narrow window; a gas fire was set into the chimney-breast. The surround looked as though it dated back to the fifties or maybe the sixties. Pride of place was given to a framed photograph of two children sitting together, obviously taken in a studio with a seaside backdrop. The ceiling and walls were stained a yellowy brown from what must have been years of cigarette smoke. A drop-leaf table stood in front of the window with a dining chair standing sentry either side. Curiously in one corner, three television sets were balanced on top of each other. Two ill-matched armchairs with threadbare coverings faced each other. The one Hannah occupied offered little comfort.

"They got rid of the chair he died in." Lucy slurped some tea from the saucer but didn't elucidate as to who "they" were.

As she had come into the tiny hall, Hannah had noticed what must be termed the scullery to the right. Hannah glanced at the red Formica topped table and two chairs against the wall. The other doors to the left must be to the bathroom and the bedroom, which, Lucy had told her, was just big enough for a bed, wardrobe and chest of drawers, was opposite. Everything was shabby but Hannah had the impression that Lucy had cleaned every inch of the place. Not a fleck of dust was to be seen. And the same might be said of Lucy. She too gave the impression of having been scrubbed and polished. Hannah noticed the roughness of her hands but the lines on her face seemed to have softened.

"Must have been traumatic for you, finding him like that."

"Nah. Seen enough dead bodies in the City. Probably a bit fresher though."

"No love lost between you then?" Hannah laughed at Lucy's expression. Then she saw the tear that Lucy hurriedly brushed away.

"You could say that."

Hannah had wondered what had led Lucy to a life of sleeping rough on the streets but in spite of having lived so publically she was a very private person. In her albeit limited experience, many of the homeless were. They each had a history, which they didn't wish to share.

Many just wanted to forget the life they'd left behind, Hannah assumed.

Lucy stood up and walked over to the rosewood sideboard above which was a framed print of Queen Elizabeth at her coronation. Opening the cupboard she brought out a half bottle of brandy and two small amber coloured glasses with gold rims. Hannah was about to decline when she noticed how pale Lucy was.

Sitting opposite each other they both sipped their drinks in silence.

"He ruined my life, didn't he." It was a bald statement of fact.

Hannah waited. But Lucy sighed deeply and finished her drink.

"The reason I asked you here," she said finally, "is I need your help."

"If I can I –

"Oh Simon Ryan said you'd be the person." Her sly smile revealed the gaps in her teeth.

"Simon?"

"How d'you think I'm staying 'ere?"

"I've no idea, Lucy. I thought you were clearing out your brother's effects."

"I am. I was. But I'm living here now. Mr Ryan got them to transfer the tenancy to me."

"Did he? But how?" Hannah had no idea who owned these flats or how they were let.

"I'm his next of kin. Anyway Mr Ryan was coming down to London and called in to see me. He went through some stuff." Lucy poured herself another shot: Hannah placed her hand over her glass, which was still almost full. "Long and the short of it, he persuaded the landlords to give me the tenancy. Don't know how. But the rent's cheap and with what the social give me now I've got a proper address, I should be able to manage it. Harry left a bit of money too."

Hannah absorbed this information. How things had changed for Lucy.

"Nothing like going to the top to get things movin'," she commented.

"I expect the landlord was impressed by your friends in high places."

"'S'pose so. Anyway if you can go through all the stuff in these envelopes it would really help. Me eyes aren't that good these days."

Hannah wondered how much Lucy could read. But she had some spare time so she could do this for her. "Am I looking for anything in particular, Lucy?"

"Not sure. But I know you'll be discreet."

Each woman smiled but for different reasons. Hannah wondered why she needed discretion. Family skeletons? "And what about your sister?"

"What sister?" Lucy regarded at her blankly.

"I'm sorry, maybe I misunderstood. When we were at Liz Rayman's funeral you told me the poem I read, Andrew Marvell's 'Mourning', was your sister's favourite."

"Blimey you've got a good memory. Better than mine."

"Useful in my line of work." Hannah had had reason to be thankful for her ability to recall complete conversations on more than one occasion.

"Well I don't remember saying that. But if I did I would have been talking about the sisters."

"The sisters?" Hannah was thrown. If there were more of them why hadn't they been contacted by the police?

"Nuns. I used to stay with the nuns. They were my sisters." Lucy obviously thought the conversation was over. "Anyway if you want to contact me there's a phone here." She pushed a piece of paper across the table. "That's the number." Lucy stood up signaling an end to their conversation. Hannah smiled at the way Lucy had taken control of the situation. She had been dismissed.

"Thanks I'll get back to you about the papers then." Hannah packed everything into her briefcase.

As she was leaving, Lucy said, "He was my twin."

"Oh Lucy I'm so sorry."

"Yeah, well he was also the reason I was on the streets." Hannah waited for an explanation but Lucy just smiled. "I'll wait to hear from you," she said as she closed the door firmly behind her guest.

Email to Simon Ryan

Dear Simon,

Have just returned from a visit to Lucy Peters who is now living in her dead brother's flat. I understand you managed to arrange that for her and also suggested that I help her go through some personal and family papers he had left. I am happy to do this for her as I have some spare time at the moment.

What I don't understand is why she was questioned – under caution, I think – by the police. I assumed the brother, Harry, had died of natural causes. But I have the feeling that was not the case? Do you know who interviewed her?

How are you and your parents?

Let me know if you know anything I should be aware of regarding Lucy.

Best wishes, Hannah.

CHAPTER SIX

The post had arrived; a few press releases and, inevitably, a few bills. At least these didn't present a problem now. She was about to start on Lucy's envelopes when something on a release she'd barely glanced at caught her eye. She read it thoroughly then, her fury barely contained, called for a cab.

"Have you seen what she's done now?"

Rory glanced up from the page proofs he was checking seeming neither surprised nor put out by the way Hannah had burst into the office. "Who?"

"That... that bitch Judy the not-so-bloody obscure?"

The news editor stared at Hannah. From his expression Hannah assumed he knew what was coming as she threw a press release across the desk. It was from a newish publishing house, Hallstone Books, announcing an amazing new thriller based on Judy Barton's own experiences as an investigative journalist.

"Isn't she under contract? Didn't she have to sign the Official Secrets Act?" Hannah was incandescent with rage. She herself had had to sign all sorts of official forms after the death of Paul Montague, her daughter's father. He hadn't committed suicide while on remand but there had been a news black out on why he had been murdered. She was also tied by her contract with *The News* although she wondered if she would stay when it came up for renewal.

Rory looked sheepish. "Judy resigned when George

refused to have her back in the London office."

Hannah flopped heavily into the chair near Rory's desk. She was furious that Judy was profiting from her relationship with Paul. And, she had to admit too, she was worried about how she would be represented in the book – presuming there was a character based on her. Judy might, of course, have written her out of history.

"Could we get an advance proof?"

"Already in hand. George got Mr Legal Eagle himself to ask for the manuscript and believe me he'll be going through it with the finest of toothcombs. George is absolutely furious and Lord Gyles isn't exactly happy so I hear. Judy may just have shot herself in the foot."

Hannah wasn't reassured. "How? She could have a bestseller on her hands plus have settled a few scores."

"Lord Gyles has various publishing interests. I think he was a financial interest in Hallstone Books."

She looked slightly mollified. "Well, I won't hold my breath."

"So, what are you doing in the office? I thought you were taking some leave?"

Hannah's face flushed. "I was but to be honest I'm at a bit of a loose end. And when I received that press release I used it as an excuse to…"

"Invite me out for lunch?"

"If you're not too busy?"

"No and I can't think of anything I'd like better. You can tell me all about your loose ends." He smiled. "I'll just finish these pages and then I'm all yours."

The Pen & Ink was busy with the usual lunchtime crowd

of journos. Rory and Hannah squeezed into a corner table with drinks. The others sitting at the table barely glanced their way. Hannah had never been more grateful for her anonymity. She was thankful to Lord Gyles and the editor Georgina Henderson for keeping her face out of the limelight and, of course, this was aided by MI5 and her signing of the Official Secrets Act.

"So what's happening with Tom?" Rory sipped his beer watching Hannah playing with her wine glass before she took a large gulp.

"He's away at the moment. Some sort of debriefing cum let's see where you'll fit in now course, I think." Hannah felt bad lying to Rory but couldn't share Tom's actual circumstances. It was too personal. Too raw.

"Is that him or you playing cards close to your chest?" Rory laughed at her expression. "Only kidding. Lighten up, Hannah."

"If only." But she did smile and some of the worry lines on her face relaxed. "I'm not sure about anything at the moment." She finished her wine. "Except being furious with Judy about her book."

Rory picked up his empty glass and pointed to Hannah's.

"Thanks, a Perrier please." She absorbed Rory's expression and laughed. "Someone mentioned I'd put on weight so I'm cutting down on the alcohol."

Left alone at the table, Hannah glanced over to the bar. She saw Rory talking to someone, then shake his head. He returned with their drinks.

"Who was that you were talking to at the bar?"

"Darren – one of the subs. Why?"

"Nothing. He just seemed familiar."

"He probably does – you must have walked past his desk a hundred times." Rory put his hand over hers. "What do you want to do about Judy?"

"Kill her?" Hannah's face paled. "I really didn't mean that. Christ after everything that's happened I joke about murder."

Rory laughed. "Especially after everything that's happened." He took a long gulp of beer. "Why don't you meet her?"

"What? Why on earth would I want to do that?"

"Show a bit of female solidarity, perhaps?"

Hannah glared at him.

"Why don't you offer her something of Paul's. You mentioned a while ago that you didn't know what to do with all his things. Give her a memento. Maybe she'll tell you about her book…"

"I don't have her contact details."

Rory snorted. "And you couldn't ask me?"

"Okay. I'll ring her. She probably won't agree to meet me."

"Well you won't know unless you ask."

Hannah gave him a withering look. They finished their drinks and left together.

"Coming back to the office?"

"May as well collect madam's telephone number." Hannah knew she had Jude to thank for telling the editor about what had been happening with Paul but the thought of having to face her made her feel sick. That woman had done her utmost to make her life a misery. Then she remembered the tip-off Jude had left on her answerphone a couple of months ago saying that someone was trying to dig up any dirt on her. She owed her for that at least. And she ought to see her before anyone started trying to block her book.

Judy sounded remarkably and uncharacteristically friendly when Hannah phoned from the office. Maybe Hannah had it all wrong about the woman.

"Why don't you pop round for a drink tomorrow evening? About sevenish?" Hannah agreed and Jude gave her an address in Islington.

What Hannah hadn't told Rory was that she had one or two things that she assumed belonged to Judy. That is if Paul hadn't been seeing someone else as well. But Hannah didn't think so. He wasn't that much of a shit.

When she left *The News* offices she was in a slightly better frame of mind. But only slightly. Having your own recent history passed off as someone else's fiction was galling.

She arrived home in time to give Elizabeth her bath. Janet looked tired.

"Is everything all right, Janet?"

The nanny's expression softened. "Yes no problems here, are there little one?" Elizabeth's little face beamed.

"No problems," she echoed and gave Janet a hug.

"Could you stay on to babysit tomorrow evening?"

"Yes, as long as I can have an hour off in the late afternoon to see to Mum."

"Of course. How is she?"

Janet shrugged. "Frustrated, tetchy, irritating and needy."

Hannah had never heard her be so critical of her parent. "I wonder what our mothers would say to each other about their daughters?"

That brought a smile to Janet's face. "I wonder." A comfortable silence stretched between the two women. "Night then."

"Night Janet. Say bye bye, Elizabeth." The toddler obliged and then flicked some bubbles at her mother bringing her back to the here and now.

After she'd put Elizabeth to bed, Hannah thought back to her visit to Paul's flat with the solicitor Neville Rogers. When they entered there was little post – mainly circulars and advertising flyers – which he leafed through then left to one side on the hall table. He answered Hannah's unspoken question. "I had the mail redirected to my office."

"Of course." Hannah felt like a voyeur. It seemed wrong for her to be here but Neville was insistent that she be there on her daughter's behalf.

The place had been surprisingly clean and tidy but then Neville said that Paul had kept on his cleaner obviously expecting his time on remand to be short-lived.

However, it was evident that apart from the cleaner, someone else had been to the apartment. It was little signs that gave the game away. Although Hannah had never been to this place she knew how Paul liked to arrange his possessions. He was very particular. His bookshelves were all wrong. Paul had had his own idiosyncratic way of organising his books. Not alphabetically by author but in the order he had read them. Fiction and nonfiction side by side. Someone had rearranged them alphabetically with a different shelf for nonfiction. A photo-frame had been broken. Hannah was surprised to see an image of Elizabeth. When or how he had obtained it, she had no idea.

The sitting room was stuffy and Neville had opened a window. The view was of a well-maintained shared garden. The room revealed no secrets. It hardly looked lived-in – there was no real sense of the owner. But she knew Paul liked to live clutter-free. Had she been part of the clutter?

Hannah hesitated at the bedroom door. Neville touched her arm. He had brought a photographer with them and he was listing an inventory of the contents into a Dictaphone. A weariness descended upon her like an unwelcome rain cloud. In all the years she'd known Paul, she had never felt so close to him as she did now in the home he had created after they had split up. A place she had never been to before. There was a faint familiarity as well as a sense of disassociation.

The bedroom recreated the one she had known and sometimes shared with him in his previous flat. The king-sized bed with the two small bedside tables. The corner shelf full of beloved trophies he'd won at school and college. The framed photo of him with some footballer she didn't recognise. He'd been so proud of it. As she stood in the doorway taking it all in she remembered the Paul she'd once known. The crinkles around his eyes when he smiled, the frown lines, the feel of the stubble on his face at the end of the day. She smiled as wave upon wave on memories broke into ripples on the surface of her mind, threatening to overwhelm her.

"Hannah?" Neville's voice broke into her thoughts. "Hannah, are you okay?"

Hannah wiped away the tears on her face and tried to smile. "Yes fine." Then she asked the question that had been on the tip of her tongue the whole time they'd been in the flat. "Don't you think it's strange we never met before? You've known Paul a lot longer but he never introduced us. We never met at a party or…"

The solicitor's face clouded. "Not strange really. We hadn't actually been in touch for some years. Paul was ace at compartmentalising his life."

"I thought all men did that."

Neville looked uncomfortable. "There was another reason…"

Hannah waited silently.

"I married the woman he was in love with."

A bolt of realisation. Paul's lack of commitment. Paul had been in love with someone else. It hadn't been anything to do with her as she'd assumed. He had made a commitment. Just not to her. It all made sense. Maybe he was hoping Neville and his wife would divorce and he'd be in with a chance?

"What's your wife's name?"

"Yvonne. Why?"

For a moment Hannah was back in Paul's previous flat. She had been flicking through his old LPs. One caught her eye as it had something written on the back: *Happy memories with Yvonne*. At the time she'd thought about asking Paul about her but decided against it. Now she knew.

"Thank you." Hannah walked into the en suite bathroom. It looked like something out of an upmarket hotel. Pure Paul. At the sink, she splashed her face with cold water. She turned to reach for a towel. And then she saw it. The woman's dressing-gown hung on the door.

For a second she felt the betrayal like a sharp kick in the stomach. Then sensibility prevailed. They had both moved on. She opened the bathroom cabinet and saw what she now expected to see – female toiletries. Clarins creams and cleansers. A small bottle of Chanel perfume.

She could sense that Neville was watching her but wisely he kept his own counsel and for that she was grateful.

"Has Judy Barton been in touch with you? Or you with her?"

For a moment Neville looked blankly at her. Then he remembered. Judy the journalist who worked at *The News*. The one who...

"No she hasn't. I didn't think there was any necessity to contact her. Paul didn't mentioned her in the instructions he left."

Hannah walked back into the bedroom. She opened the drawers of the bedside table on the left side. Paul always slept to the right or he did when she was with him. The bottom drawer contained some women's underwear. The top drawer revealed a miscellany of clutter: a necklace, a lipstick, some restaurant receipts, a paperback, some painkillers and a small box she didn't open.

Hannah pulled the drawer out and tipped the contents into an empty cardboard box along with the underwear then she went back into the bathroom and collected the toiletries and the dressing gown. She glanced around. Satisfied she had everything.

"I'll return these items." Her tone broached no dissent. She closed the box and Neville labelled it.

They went back into the sitting room.

"Is there anything you want to take now as a personal memento..." he caught Hannah's glare. "Perhaps something for Elizabeth? For when she's older?"

Hannah bit back the remark she was about to make. She knew she had no right to deprive her daughter of access to something of her father's. "Is there anything you would suggest?"

There was a sheepishness about his expression for a second or two. "I kept his watch, a ring and a silver chain he wore ..."

"Thank you." She paused. "Perhaps as Paul's executor and a trustee you could keep hold of anything you think Paul might have liked his daughter to have?"

It was the first time Neville had heard her use the word daughter in relation to Paul. He could sense how much it had cost Hannah. "Of course."

The photographer had left earlier. Neville looked around. The flat would be easy to sell and Hannah hadn't been difficult as he thought she might be.

"I don't know about you, but I could do with a drink and something to eat. Fancy joining me?"

Hannah was about to refuse then realised how hungry she was.

"Thank you."

Neville closed the windows and locked the doors as they left. There would be no need for her to return.

•

Thinking back to her meal with Neville when he'd turned out to be surprisingly good company, Hannah realised how hungry she was. She made herself a sandwich and switched on the TV. She'd been recording *The Singing Detective*, which was being shown again after Dennis Potter's death the month before, and decided to watch another episode. She was soon engrossed in the world portrayed by Michael Gambon and Joanne Whalley, a far cry from her own. And a welcome retreat.

CHAPTER SEVEN

The next morning Hannah received an email from Simon Ryan:

Dear Hannah,

How lovely to hear from you!

I was contacted by the police when Lucy was questioned about finding her brother's body and arranged for a solicitor to be with her. I was also able to help her acquire the tenancy of her brother's flat. I think the agents were terrified I might delve into the legalities of some of their activities! It was actually quite fun.

Lucy was questioned under caution. There's a question mark over Harry's demise although I haven't heard anything further from the solicitor in London. I don't suppose the brother's death rates that highly in the Met's priorities. I believe our old friend DS Benton interviewed her. Apparently he and the woman police officer were kind to her but I haven't heard anything more.

On a personal note, my parents' health has deteriorated since Patrick's murder and they are very sad as can be imagined. I miss him terribly...

I'm hoping to be in London soon so perhaps we could meet up for dinner and compare notes? And, of course, it would be lovely to see you!

Best wishes, Simon

Going through Lucy's family papers reminded Hannah of when Lady Celia Rayman had asked her to sort her dead daughter's papers. Her close friend Liz's affairs were complicated and had led to the exposure of a syndicate trafficking Somali girls. Lucy's envelopes of papers were far less numerous and much more personal. There was the marriage certificate of the parents Nancy and Bill. Then there were the birth certificates for Lucy and her twin brother Harry. Their father had registered them. So Lucy was sixty-three years old. She looked much older. They had been christened at St Peter's in the Walworth Road. Dated much later, when the twins were thirteen, was another birth certificate. A child called Edward, registered by their mother. Hannah couldn't find a baptismal certificate. Not that that meant anything. It could have been lost. But it was strange. Nancy, their mother, seemed to have kept so many miscellaneous papers and receipts as well as tiny black and white photos, faded and yellowed at the edges. Hannah could just make out the twins in some of them. There seemed to be no photos of Edward.

Hannah wondered when the parents had died. Lucy had mentioned that Harry had been given his smaller flat when their mother had died. So presumably the father had died first. But there was nothing to indicate when this was. Hannah found the death certificate for Nancy and an in memoriam card stating her ashes had been buried at Streatham Park Crematorium. She'd been in her twenties when she had the twins. Odd that Harry should have carried on living with her and not Lucy. Why hadn't he married or just left home? Mothers and sons, Hannah thought. Some women never let their male children go. She wondered if she'd react differently to a baby boy.

In amongst all the paraphenalia Hannah found an old address book. As she flipped through it a piece of folded tissue paper slipped out. Inside was a lock of hair tied with a tiny thin ribbon. She realised that it had fallen out of the page devoted to E. She examined the list of names. She almost missed an entry for Edward which someone had tried to rub out. Hannah couldn't make out the address.

She put some tracing paper on top of the page then gently rubbed a soft pencil over it. It looked as though part of the address was something 'House' and 'Wiltshire'. There was undoubtedly a light box, which would give her a better idea at *The News* offices. She'd check it out. But what had happened to Lucy's younger brother, Edward?

Scraps of paper with barely legible writing Hannah put to one side. She paused. Her neck was stiff and a headache was threatening. She felt slightly sick and went downstairs to the kitchen for a glass of water. As she had the house to herself she decided to sit in the garden, for a change of air. The scent of roses and lavender and the warmth of the sun had a soporific effect.

"Mama, Mama!" Hannah struggled upright. She had fallen asleep in a deckchair.

"Hello my gorgeous girl – did you have a lovely time at the park?"

"Swim swim!"

Hannah could see Janet was looking at her strangely. Simple mistake. "Yes of course swimming," she replied as Elizabeth clambered up on to her lap. Placing her chubby hands either side of Hannah's face she leaned forwards and kissed her lips.

"D'you fancy a coffee, Hannah?"

"No thanks, but could you get me a glass of water while I sort out this little minx?" Elizabeth squealed as her mother tickled her.

Janet returned with the water and a drink for Elizabeth. "I'll just go and rinse the swimming things. Anything else you need me to do?"

Hannah looked preoccupied. "Yes, why don't you bring a drink and sit in the sunshine with us for a while?"

Janet smiled and joined them after hanging out the swimming costumes.

"How's your mother?"

"Much the same. Why?"

"I was just wondering about her. How old is she?"

Janet laughed. "Sixty-one but don't tell her I told you. She's precious about her age. God knows why."

Similar age to Lucy. "I wonder if she'd talk to me about her early life around here... I'm researching a story and she might have some good background knowledge."

"I'm sure she would. And she'd love to meet you."

Hannah felt a twinge of guilt. Janet's mother's disability meant she couldn't get out much. Probably didn't have too many visitors either. "Okay when you get home ask her is she'd mind me phoning her."

Janet looked askance.

"To arrange a good time to visit her." Hannah smiled at Elizabeth and blew a raspberry on her tummy. "We don't want these daughters taking over all the arrangements do we now?" She smiled up at Janet. "Do you want to get off now and I'll see you later for babysitting?"

CHAPTER EIGHT

Hannah awkwardly descended the wrought iron spiral steps to Judy's basement flat and clasped the railing. The entrance was set back under the steps on the ground level so it was quite dark although she could see a light in a window. The steps turned once more and Hannah was facing an open door. The evening was still warm and the scent of roses from the pots by the door gave a reassurance but surely Judy wouldn't be so careless of security?

Hannah rang the bell. She glanced at her watch. 7.00pm. The exact time Judy had invited her. No answer. She rang again. "Judy are you there?"

She pushed the door further open and called again. Nothing. Her gut reaction told her to leave – now. All her instincts as a journalist propelled her forward into the flat. The hall was minute and she opened the door into what transpired to be the sitting room and stood in mute horror. The place had been turned upside down. Every drawer opened, contents spilled. Cushions removed from the sofa. Books thrown to the floor. Curiously a vase of roses stood proud and upright, a beacon of normality in the volcanic mess.

"Judy?"

Hannah backed out of the sitting room. She opened the door opposite, which revealed a bedroom that also seemed as though it had been hit by a hurricane. But no Judy. Equally the bathroom and kitchen were devoid of their owner. Imagining the worst case scenario that Judy had been abducted or ... Hannah pulled out her mobile phone and pressed 999.

After asking to be put through to the police, she gave the address and continued, "It looks as though there's been a break-in and the person I'm here to see is missing ..." Hannah ended the call and wondered what to do next. She realised she'd already contaminated the crime scene with her fingerprints, so she resisted the impulse to sit on the sofa in case she disturbed anything. She did, however, take some photos while she waited then stood in the hall and checked her watch.

"Fucking hell, Hannah, what the hell are you playing at?"

It took her a few seconds to absorb the sound behind her. She turned to see Judy standing there full of righteous indignation. "What have you done to my flat?"

"Judy! Thank God. I arrived a few minutes ago and the door was ajar. When you didn't answer the doorbell, I came in and saw all this."

"A likely story. What were you searching for? My manuscript?"

"No!" Hannah was aghast at the accusation.

The sound of a siren grew louder then silence. Hannah could see a blue light flashing above the railings at street level. Heavy footsteps descended the spiral staircase. Then two uniformed officers appeared in the doorway.

"Thank heavens you're here." Judy turned the full power of her smile on them. "This ... this woman has ... has..." Judy gave an elegant sweep of her hand to encompass the scene and burst into a torrent of tears.

It had taken Hannah an hour at the police station to convince the officers she wasn't the perpetrator of the mess at Judy's flat.

"Ask her if anything is missing," she demanded.

The two officers exchanged a glance, which Hannah couldn't interpret.

"A scenes of crime officer is at the flat with her now, Ms Weybridge, and we have your fingerprints so..."

The other officer looked up from a sheet of paper in front of him. "Does Ms Barton have a grudge against you?"

Hannah snorted. "You could say that but it's a long story. She –"

Just then the door opened and DS Benton walked in. Hannah's mood hit rock bottom. Mike Benton would have a field day with her. He was smiling. Never a good sign in her experience.

"Well, well, well – breaking and entering. Not your normal style Hannah..."

It took a moment for her to realise his smile was genuine and he was joking.

"I'll give you a lift home." He nodded at the two uniformed officers. "I think you'll find this has all been an elaborate hoax. Ms Barton thought she could drum up some publicity for her forthcoming book by implying that Ms Weybridge broke into and trashed her flat. She is deeply ashamed at having wasted police time and will be making a generous donation to a charity of our choice."

Hannah followed Mike out of the interview room. "How did you know?"

Mike swiped his security pass and opened the external door for her. "You're in our system. Your name flags up..."

Hannah wasn't sure whether to be relieved or worried at this. For the time being relief reigned supreme. "I always seem to have you to thank for rescuing me, these days."

Mike harrumphed. "Just don't make a habit of it." He looked embarrassed.

"You don't have to drive me home, Mike. I can get a cab."

"It's on my way." She was relieved when he approached an unmarked car and unlocked the door.

"You seem different. A lot happier these days." Hannah fastened her seatbelt as Mike manoeuvred the car out of the car park.

"I am." He didn't elaborate.

Hannah settled back into the seat. "A year ago I'd never been in a police car. Now I seem to make a habit of it."

Mike glanced at her. "The things people will do for a free ride." He realised his mistake as soon as the words were out of his mouth. Hannah's face was ashen. "Sorry I didn't mean to make light of –"

Hannah took a deep relaxing breath. "Don't apologise for heaven's sake." She turned towards him and he saw the unshed tears. "And don't be nice to me DS Benton. Bad habit." Her attempt at a joke almost worked. She swallowed hard and searched for a tissue in her handbag.

Benton drove on in silence. She had never thought of him as a sensitive man – far from it – but she was grateful that he was showing this hitherto hidden side of himself now.

"How's DI Turner?" she asked when she felt she could trust her voice to sound normal.

"Same as ever. I'm surprised you haven't seen her. You two seem to get along and you have Tom Jordan in common."

"What on earth do you mean?"

Hannah's stricken expression made Benton immediately regret his comment. "Only that she trained with him and you and he…" He left the sentence unfinished.

"Have you heard anything?"

"About DI Jordan?" Hannah nodded. "Nothing at all. But that's usually a good sign," he said as they turned into her road and drew up outside her house.

"Don't let that bitch Judy Barton get to you Hannah. You're made of sterner stuff."

"Am I? Wish I could be sure about that." She got out of the car and leaned in before shutting the door. "Thanks Mike." For a moment they stared at each other in a rare moment of mutual understanding. Then he nodded and put the car into gear as she closed the door. But she noticed he didn't immediately drive off but was waiting until she was safely inside her home.

Janet turned off the television programme she had been watching when Hannah came in. "How was your … Hannah you look awful. What's happened?"

Hannah flopped down on the other sofa. "It was a set-up. She had me arrested for apparently breaking and entering her flat."

Janet looked appalled. Before she could say anything, Hannah continued, "Fortunately I am on some police system and my arrest was flagged up. Sergeant Benton turned up to sort it out and brought me home."

"Jesus what an absolute bitch."

"Got it in one." Hannah smiled weakly. "Thanks for being here, Janet. If you don't mind I'm going to have a shower. I want to get the stench of that woman off of me –" she took in Janet's expression – "metaphorically speaking that is."

Janet picked up her belongings. "See you tomorrow. Sleep well." She let herself out and Hannah double locked the door and switched on the alarm before going upstairs. All she wanted to do was cry but by the time she got into bed, tiredness took over and sleep prevailed.

CHAPTER NINE

The next morning Hannah had already fired off an email to Rory about the events at Judy's flat and was thinking about phoning Sheila, Janet's mother, when the telephone rang. Hannah let the answerphone pick up until she heard the librarian's voice.

"Hi Natalie, sorry I've been screening my calls. How are you?"

"Feeling much better, thanks. Back at work and it's almost as though that poor man didn't die here. I wondered if you have the time for a chat? Maybe lunch?"

They agreed to meet in The Plough. Hannah gazed out of the window watching the branches of a neighbour's tree sway in the breeze. Another sunny day. It made her think of Tom and their time away together. What was happening with him now? She hoped he'd conquer his demons or at least find ways to control them. She looked at her watch, time to make another call.

It was warm enough to take their drinks and ploughman's lunches into the garden at the rear of The Plough.

A couple of young mothers were sitting on the grass with their toddlers. Hannah and Natalie moved to the shaded tables.

"Thanks for your kindness the other day."

Hannah sipped her spritzer. "No need to thank me. And the minicab was courtesy of *The News*." She laughed. "Your face! You look as though you've supped with the devil."

Natalie blushed. "No not at all! Anyway, the police haven't said anything about the man who died but he was rather interesting."

"In what way?"

"He was over from Australia and was trying to trace some family connections. He had a couple of names of people who he thought had been born locally. I suggested checking baptism records with local churches as a good starting point and, of course, he'd have to go to Somerset House."

"And did he find who he was looking for?"

"No idea really. He was researching newspapers dating back to just after the war but I don't know why."

Both women concentrated on their bread and cheese. One of the toddlers on the grass let out a scream. Both mothers picked up their offspring one of whom had a badly cut knee and went marching into the bar. Hannah watched them and wondered what sort of mother she was enjoying lunch with Nathalie while her daughter...

"There was something about him," Nathalie interrupted her thoughts. "He looked lost. Hurt. Sad. I felt he was carrying a great burden."

"Sounds rather fanciful." Hannah realised how that might sound. "Sorry, that wasn't meant to be a criticism."

Nathalie smiled. "I know and point taken. It's just that I can't help feeling that he may have been killed to stop him finding his family."

"Why on earth would anyone do that?"

"People do strange things to preserve the status quo." Hannah remained silent.

"He asked for some papers to be photocopied and I

still had them when he died. I gave the originals to the police today but –" she delved into her voluminous bag – "I thought you might like the copies. Just in case." Natalie handed her a large brown envelope.

"In case of what?"

"I don't know really. It's just a gut feeling that I have. And I'd trust you to do whatever was necessary."

"Would I?" Hannah smiled to deflect the implied criticism. She glanced at her watch. "Sorry I have to be somewhere else soon." She tucked the envelope into her bag. Her life lately seemed to be made up of people passing her papers in envelopes.

"And I must return to my duties."

They left the pub together. "Thanks again for your kindness."

Hannah hugged her. "A pleasure. See you soon." Then she went across the road to buy some flowers for Janet's mother.

Although Hannah knew that Janet lived with her mother nearby – it was one of the reasons the nanny was keen on the job, to be near her mother in case of an emergency – she had never thought to walk past her home to take a look. The Lordship Lane end of Friern Road wasn't a route that she took on her local walks. It was however near to the pub where she'd had lunch with Nathalie.

Within a few minutes she'd arrived at the mansion block of flats and rang the doorbell for number 3. As she expected given Sheila's disability, it took her some time to answer the door but when she did, Hannah was taken by surprise. Her only thoughts about Sheila had been coloured by her daughter's acerbic comments from time to time. Hannah knew she was disabled by rheumatoid arthritis and could, according to Janet, be tetchy and demanding. This was not her first impression.

Sheila was wearing a bright summer dress with a pink and green floral design and her grey curly hair framed her face, which was well made up. Her lipstick matched her nail varnish. Slightly bent forward, her disfigured hands resting on the Zimmer frame handles, Sheila smiled widely.

"Come in Hannah. So lovely to meet you at last."

Hannah stepped into the wide hall and noticed a wheelchair folded against the wall. "Thank you for inviting me, Sheila." She gently shook the older woman's hand and noticed how soft her skin was. "These are for you. Shall I..." Hannah was about to suggest she took the flowers into the kitchen for her to put them in water but Sheila took them from her, inhaling their fragrance for a moment, then placing them into the basket attached to the front of her frame.

"Thank you. I love roses and the pink matches my dress. Go into the sitting room while I put these in water."

Hannah went as directed into a large, bright room. One wall was covered in framed photos of Janet and another child and adult she assumed to be her sister, taken throughout their lives. A pictorial history. However there seemed to be a couple of frames missing judging by the spaces with a slight dust marks within them.

Hannah walked over to take a closer look. Janet and

her sister were very similar physically. On a low bookcase, two photo-frames had been placed face down. Hannah picked up one then the other, replacing it quickly as Sheila came into the room pushing a tea trolley set with a coffee pot, mugs, plates and a fruitcake.

Sheila smiled, nodding at the wall. "Janet hates having all these photos on show but I love them. Sometimes I just sit in my chair and take a journey back in time when I wasn't riddled with this arthritis." She pointed to an armchair for Hannah to sit in. "Would you do the honours, dear, and pour the coffee. My hands are a bit stiff." Hannah wondered how she'd managed with the kettle but perhaps in her kitchen she had gadgets to help her.

"Help yourself to some cake." Hannah served them both a slice.

"You must be glad that Janet is here for you, Sheila."

Hannah thought Janet's mother's expression meant she'd taken the comment as a criticism and was about to elaborate but Sheila spoke first.

"I worry about her. She spends all of her time either caring for your child or me. She has no life of her own. My other daughter – well I don't see her from one month's end to the next. And she's pretty secretive about her life. But at least she has one. Poor Janet has to put up with me when the pain gets too much and I get cranky and to put not too fine a point on it she's been through some rough times with you."

"I know and I am eternally grateful to her. I'm so sorry you've had so much extra worry."

Sheila waved a hand at her. "If Janet hadn't been

involved that time with the explosion, I'd have found it all rather exciting. I think she does too."

Hannah tried to think of recent events from another perspective. Perhaps some would view it as exciting. She was exhausted by it.

"Anyway you didn't come here to talk about that, I gather. So how can I help?"

Hannah fished out her small Dictaphone from her bag. "Would you mind if I record our conversation? Helps me concentrate on what we're discussing."

Sheila looked a bit doubtful. "I hate hearing myself on those things."

"You won't have to listen to it and no one else will either. Only me."

Janet's mother nodded and settled herself back in her chair.

"You've lived in the area all of your life, haven't you and –"

"Apart from being evacuated during the war. We went to somewhere in Wiltshire I think it was, mum, me and my two brothers. Dad was in the army and when we returned our home had been bombed – a pile of rubble – and we were given a prefab when dad was demobbed."

"It must have been difficult to keep track of people in those days."

"Oh it was. Sometimes, according to my mum, people deliberately went awol. The blitz offered them an escape route." She paused to drink her tea. "Some of them came back, others disappeared for ever. My mum's sister lost her son."

"I'm sorry I..."

"Oh Derek didn't die. Well he might have by now, I suppose. No he disappeared from a children's home he'd been put in while his mother tried to sort out accommodation for them."

Hannah could feel the hairs prickling on the back of her neck.

"They tried to say he'd died but she demanded to see the death certificate. If I remember correctly from what my mum told me he'd been shipped out to Australia on some Child Migration Project. Terrible business."

"Did that happen a lot, do you think?"

"More than people would admit to. My husband reckoned there'd be a backlash. I'm surprised he was wrong. He rarely was about these things."

"I wouldn't be too sure of that," Hannah said almost to herself. "What did your husband do for a living?"

"He was a ... he worked in security."

Hannah smiled and looked over at a photo of Sheila, her husband and two young girls. "You must miss him."

Sheila laughed. "Not really. He was never around that much and the woman he went off with leads him a right old dance. Divine retribution."

Hannah finished her coffee. She had always assumed that Janet's father was dead. "Going back to your relative. Do you know of any others who lost track of their children like that?"

"Not personally. My aunt met a few others. When they tried to trace their children they were met with obstacles all the time. And she didn't have the money to pursue it. She never forgot him though. She had two more boys later but there was always a sadness in her."

Hannah turned off the Dictaphone. "Perhaps we could talk again?"

"Anytime. I don't go out much. Sometimes it's too much of a faff trying to get a taxi that will take a wheelchair. But at the weekends Janet and I go out. She's a good daughter."

Hannah considered her for a moment. "Is there anything I can do before I go?"

"No dear, but I would like you to investigate what happened to those children. If you have the time."

"They'll be adults now…"

"Yes and maybe they are looking for their families."

Hannah thought of the man who had died in the library. "Perhaps they are. I'll let you know if I uncover anything."

Hannah had plenty to think about after her talk with Sheila. As she walked home she considered her options. Janet appeared slightly wary when she let herself in.

"Everything go okay with Mum?"

Hannah smiled. "Yes she was very informative. Lots to think about. How was soft play?"

That evening Hannah opened the envelope Nathalie had given her. A dead man's thoughts, photocopied. Sheets of innocuous annotated notes. Certainly nothing to be murdered for if that was the case.

Jeff Collins had obviously found his original birth registration and had photocopied the copy of that certificate. Alongside was a copy of a certificate of Australian nationalisation, which had been registered in Queensland.

There was an address for the Christian Brotherhood of the Holy Pilgrims, which according to the notes ran some sort of children's home. Hannah paused. She had assumed that children sent out to Australia on the Child Migration Scheme were adopted by families. Obviously that was not always the case.

There was a list of names but nothing to say why they were listed, addresses which were followed by a question mark. In all Jeff Collins didn't seem as though he had made much progress in finding his English family. A few scraps of paper to show for his life.

Hannah checked her emails. A single word message from Rory: SORRY.

But no apology from Judy. Why had she expected one?

CHAPTER TEN

Something was nagging at the back of her mind. Lucy's family documents such as they were, gave little away about their actual lives. In the front of Nancy Peters's address book she had written her own address. The home presumably Lucy had once shared with her family. She decided to go there and see if any of the neighbours remembered them and more importantly what they recalled.

The address was only about ten minutes' walk from where Lucy now lived. Hannah arrived in front of a newly painted door with a gleaming brass knocker in the shape of a lion's head. She had decided honesty (and perhaps a few notes changing hands) might be her best policy. No one answered her knock so she moved on to the flat the other side of the one Lucy's family had lived in. This time she rang a bell, anticipating a wait, but the door was opened immediately by a young woman wearing a smart linen suit and a questioning smile. Hannah was thrown. She'd expected an elderly occupant – someone in her eighties.

"Hi, have you come to see my gran?"

Hannah was about to reply but the young woman continued, "She's in the sitting room. She could do with some company." And with that she left.

Hannah stood where she was. Uncertain. She should take advantage of the situation but she was stunned by the young woman's casual invitation. Clearly she was expecting someone else.

"Hello? If you're coming in, come in and close the door behind you," a querulous voice called from within.

Hannah did as she was bid and walked a few paces down the hall into the sitting room where a woman with white hair styled like the Queen Mother's, sat by an open window where she'd been feeding the birds. A few pigeons hovered on the windowsill in the hope of more.

"Hello Mrs Ford." – she'd found the names of the tenants on the electoral register – "My name is Hannah and I'm from *The News...*"

"What the paper? What are you doing here? I was expecting the girl who comes and reads to me. My granddaughter's just left." The woman who, Hannah realised, must be nearly blind, looked agitated.

"Yes I met her at the door. She told me to come through."

"Did she now. So, what do you want?" Her tone had changed to irritated, belligerent.

Taking a deep breath Hannah decided on the direct approach. "I was wondering if you remembered Nancy and Bill Peters who used to live next door."

"Of course I do. Just because I have difficulty seeing doesn't mean I've lost my marbles as well."

"I would never think that. I just wasn't sure how long you've lived here." Hannah knew but didn't want to upset the woman further.

Mrs Ford's fingers stroked the oilcloth on the table she was sitting at. Suddenly she smiled. "If you want to know more you might as well sit down, I suppose."

Hannah sat on the chair facing the woman. "Come closer." Hannah did. "Give me your hand." The woman stroked her left hand. "Not married then?"

Hannah laughed. "No."

"Nor's my granddaughter. Career girl, or so she says. Works in a travel agent's."

"Sounds fun." Hannah smiled but wanted to bring the conversation back to Lucy's family. At the same time she didn't want to alienate Mrs Ford. "Did you know them well? Nancy and Bill Peters?"

"Nancy and I were friendly after a fashion. Not him though. He did a runner years ago when the twins were small. Good riddance, I thought. So did Nancy."

"And they only had the two children?" Hannah was fishing.

"They were enough, I can tell you. Always up to mischief. Lucy was a pretty little thing. She left home early. Not like that mummy's boy of a son of hers. He stayed. Anyway when Nancy died a few years ago he had to move to a smaller flat. Waste of space, that one."

"What makes you say that?"

"He just was." The old woman seemed lost in thought. "I always wondered what happened to Lucy, though."

"Why?"

"She disappeared for a while. Then when she came back she was different. She looked so sad." She seemed lost in a reverie then pulled herself back. "Why d'you want to know all this?"

Hannah took her hand. "I'm sorry to tell you this, Mrs Ford, Harry died a few weeks ago. The police think he may have been killed."

There was a silence.

"I know you shouldn't speak ill of the dead but he

probably had it coming to him," Mrs Ford said at last. "He had a vicious tongue on him when he'd had a drink or two and he upset people. He was nasty to his mother. I used to hear them arguing. The language he used. Too full of himself by far, that one."

"And Lucy?"

"Lucy? I think she became a nun."

"A nun?"

"Yes a nun. Leastways that was what her mother said." A sparrow tapped on the window then settled on the ledge with a loud chirrup. The woman put her hand into a box beside her and held out the food. The sparrow hopped onto her finger and nibbled his fill before giving a chirrup of thanks and goodbye.

Mrs Ford turned her attention to inside the room. "Sorry I haven't been much help have I?"

"Good background info." Hannah paused she didn't want to offend the woman but... "Is there anything you need or I can get for you?"

Mrs Ford thought for a moment; a cheeky smile appeared on her face. "Could you get me one of them talking books? The girl who comes isn't a great reader."

"I can certainly do that for you. Who's your favourite author?"

"Catherine Cookson. Love her books and that Wilbur Smith he knows how to tell a tale."

Hannah reached over and touched the woman's hand. "Done. And thanks for all your help. Can I leave you my card in case you remember anything?"

"Nah, won't be able to see it. Here –" she passed Hannah a large exercise book – "write your name and number in there, really big." Hannah did so. She took the book back from her and peered at the page. "That'll do. I can see that." She smiled lopsidedly.

As Hannah was leaving the block of flats she caught in her peripheral vision the silhouette of a man who seemed to be staring straight at her which was daft as she couldn't see his face. Probably her imagination playing tricks.

It was such a lovely day that she walked over Waterloo Bridge and into the Strand to find a bookshop that sold talking books. She bought the Mallen Trilogy and contemplated having them delivered to Mrs Ford but decided on balance she'd be better doing so herself so retraced her steps. On Waterloo Bridge she paused and took in her favourite view of St Paul's and The National Theatre. Such a contrast in buildings. She wondered idly if Wren would have agreed with Prince Charles who had once likened the latter to a nuclear power station. The sun on her face made her appreciate what it must be like cooped up in a small flat all day – for Mrs Ford and Sheila.

She carried on walking and approached St John's. The doors were open so, after a moment's hesitation, she ran up the steps and went inside. The extreme drop in temperature made her shiver and it took her eyes a moment to adjust to the change in light. In the silence, conversations and thoughts she'd had here echoed in her mind. As she paused under the gallery, a voice seemingly coming from nowhere asked, "Well, well, well I wondered how long it would take you to find me here."

She felt a presence behind her, a cool breath on her

skin, as someone pressed something into her neck. Her knees buckled and she was grabbed under her arms as everything descended into darkness.

Her head ached and her mouth felt dry. She opened her eyes for a second and dizziness made her close them. She tried again, and blinked gradually focusing on two concerned faces peering at her. She tried to sit up.

"No don't move dear, just stay still for a few moments." The woman's voice sounded concerned but calm. "You gave us quite a fright. Do you want us to call an ambulance?"

"Sorry?" Hannah moved her legs to the ground and sat up. She had been stretched out on a bench at the side of the church. "What on earth am I doing here?"

The two women exchanged a glance. "We found you here a few minutes ago. We'd been in the vestry and came out to find you here." She handed Hannah a glass of water. As she went to take it a strange smell wafted from her.

"Perhaps you just had a bit too much to drink?"

Hannah shook her head. "No I haven't had a drink. I came in here on a whim. I knew Father Patrick."

"There," the other woman said with a note of triumph in her voice. "I told you I recognised her from somewhere."

"So you did." She smiled at Hannah. "And I remember you at the Cathedral for Father Patrick's interment."

"Yes." The fog was clearing from Hannah's mind. "There was someone in here. A man. He said something to me and then... and then I must have passed out."

"Are you sure you didn't have a drink too many?"

"No and I've no idea why I smell of alcohol. Is my bag here?" She was handed her briefcase and the bag containing the talking books she'd bought for Mrs Ford. Opening it she was astonished to see a half bottle of gin – half empty. The two women tittered. "That is not mine." She was about to touch it then took out a paper tissue. Carefully she picked the bottle and, removing the talking books, put it into the plastic bag. "I'll get that checked," she muttered to herself. She checked through the contents of her bag – nothing seemed to be missing although her notebook was not in its usual place. So who had she disturbed and why had he done this to her?

"Are you sure you saw no one else in here?"

The two women exchanged an uncomfortable glance. "No we were… we were having a cup of tea in the vestry." They still didn't look convinced that she hadn't been drinking.

"Right. I'd better get home. Thank you for the water and your concern."

Hannah was furious. This church was bad news for her. There was always something awful associated with it. Carefully – she still felt a bit wobbly and those women were watching her – she made her way outside into the sunshine.

She hailed a black cab on Waterloo Road. She was going straight home. She'd send Mrs Ford her books by courier. As the taxi slowed down at the Elephant and Castle, she peered out of the window at people queuing for buses. Ordinary people going about everyday lives.

Why couldn't hers be less complicated?

Once home and in her study, Hannah rang Claudia. She wasn't there but she was put through to DS Benton.

"I've a favour to ask."

"Oh yes…" Benton wasn't going to make it easy for her.

"Could you… could you check a bottle for fingerprints for me and see if you have any matches?"

Benton remained silent.

"I was attacked – no that's too strong a word – something happened to me in St John's Waterloo. I must have passed out and when I came to, I reeked of gin and a half-empty bottle was in my bag."

"You didn't touch it?"

"No I lifted it out with a handkerchief and put it in a bag. I could courier it over to you."

There was a silence. "Okay – you owe me one."

"More than one, Mike. Thank you."

"And I'll need to log this Hannah." He didn't expect her to reply and she rung off. He decided to visit the church in question.

After hanging up, Hannah rang the courier service. Carefully wrapping the half-empty bottle of gin, she then placed it in a jiffy bag, glad to see the back of it with its embarrassing memories. But what had caused her to faint? And who was that man? She wondered about phoning her GP but decided the whole episode sounded far-fetched. However she needed to be on her guard. Whoever it was wanted to discredit her. Why?

DS Benton discovered nothing new about the attack on Hannah at St John's in Waterloo. The vicar knew nothing of the incident. Obviously the two women hadn't mentioned it. If it hadn't been for the half-bottle of gin, Benton might have thought nothing had happened. However Hannah Weybridge was not fanciful and from what he knew of her she wouldn't have gone to such elaborate lengths to draw attention to herself. He'd wait to see what, if anything, fingerprints came up with. After the fiasco with Judy Barton, Benton was beginning to wonder how many other people Hannah had upset.

CHAPTER ELEVEN

It had rained overnight and was slightly cooler as Hannah trudged up the stairs to number 39. She wondered how Lucy was coping with life within walls. Was it a blessing or did she feel penned in?

Lucy opened the door as soon as she rang the bell.

"Come in luv, you look all-in."

"Thanks for that compliment." Hannah followed Lucy into the sitting room. It felt different somehow although Hannah couldn't have said why. Clearly Lucy was making this her home now. "I brought you these." She handed over a bag of toiletries.

"These look posh. You been robbing hotel rooms?"

Hannah laughed. "No I still get a lot of samples to test and write about. Thought you might like to try some of them."

"Thanks." Lucy spent a moment or two examining at the various jars and tubes.

"How are you finding living here?"

"Fine. Would you like some coffee? Or something stronger?"

"A glass of water, please." While Lucy disappeared into the kitchen, Hannah noticed that she'd opened out the drop-leaf table. Presumably so they could use it to go through the papers. Hannah sat down and took the envelopes from her bag. She was just arranging the papers as Lucy returned with Hannah's water and a cup of tea for herself.

"So did you find anything interesting?" Lucy's

expression was unreadable.

Hannah rearranged some pieces of paper. "Depends what you're expecting, I suppose. There's no death certificate for your father–"

"He did a runner years ago," Lucy said confirming what Hannah had learned from the neighbour. "Don't suppose he's still alive though."

Fathers, Hannah thought. Then thought of Elizabeth who would never have the opportunity to know hers now and a chill ran through her. "What happened to your brother? Edward?"

Lucy looked at her blankly.

"Maybe you knew him as Ted or Eddy"

Lucy shook her head. "Nope. Never had another brother. Only ever me and Harry." Exactly what Mrs Ford had said.

All manner of scenarios tumbled into Hannah's mind. But the twins had been thirteen when Edward was born so they must have been aware that their mother was pregnant.

"He was born when you and Harry were thirteen…" She wondered if the years of living rough, alcohol and poor health had wiped out Lucy's memory.

"Nope and me dad wasn't around then."

"Maybe your mum had another man?"

The question produced a raucous laugh. "Nah she hated men. All men. Except Harry, of course. He was her blue-eyed boy."

"And he never married?"

Lucy shook her head. "She saw to that."

"How?"

"Dunno really. He had a girl once but then she disappeared and that was that. Harry carried on living with Mum."

"And you didn't?" Hannah had to ask the question that felt so intrusive – even for a journalist.

"No I didn't." Lucy poured some tea from her cup into the saucer and slurped loudly.

"And this brother? Edward?"

"I told you there was only me and Harry."

Hannah sipped her water, waiting. Through the open window she could hear children playing football on a patch of grass. In the room a clock marked the passage of time with a loud tick. Lucy said nothing more. Hannah watched fascinated as a range of emotions played across the older woman's face. Without saying a word she got up and left the room. Hannah sat still as the minutes lengthened. A bee buzzed into the room, then presumably seeing nothing of interest left. Hannah felt so tired. The flush of the toilet and then the bathroom taps running alerted her to Lucy's imminent return.

Hannah studied her face, which bore all the signs that she'd been crying. She went to the sideboard and brought out the brandy and two small gold-rimmed glasses as she had done on Hannah's last visit.

Lucy swigged her drink in one gulp then poured another. She raised her face and Hannah saw the tears in her eyes. "They told me my baby had been born dead."

Hannah reached out and clasped Lucy's hand.

Hannah managed to piece together some of Lucy's story told in short bursts between tots of brandy. Lucy had got pregnant – she didn't go into details but she was so young and didn't know what was happening to her body. She had only had one period and she hadn't been prepared for that. She had thought she was dying, bleeding to death; her knowledge of biology was sketchy. When her mother had discovered she was six months pregnant she was sent off to a place in the country. Lucy didn't know where.

"The nuns were really kind. All the girls there had to work in the laundry or the gardens but it was nicer than being at school and we still did some lessons." A smile played around Lucy's lips. "I loved being there. I felt safe. My mum visited now and again. Not often. But when my time came she was there for me." She paused to refill her glass and waved the bottle in Hannah's direction.

"No thanks." Hannah had not drunk any of her first glass. "Don't go on if it's too painful."

Lucy's laugh was frightening. "Having a baby was painful. Some of the other girls who'd had theirs warned me but I wouldn't believe them. My mum said it was a punishment on me for my sin."

"What was?"

"The pain and the baby being born dead. I don't remember much but afterwards I was told I'd never be able to have children. I was ill for some time then Mum brought me back to London." She sipped her drink. "How could she have lied to me like that?" She sniffed as one huge tear rolled towards her nose.

"D'you think we'd ever be able to find him. Do you think we could find Edward?"

"I don't know, Lucy. We've got so little to go on." She

remembered the rubbed out entry in the address book. "But we could try. We have the birth certificate so that's a start." She held Lucy's hand. "But if he was adopted there's probably little we can do to trace him."

"Gawd I can't get my head round this. First my brother's dead then I find I could have a son somewhere." She shook her head and poured another drink.

Hannah collected her things together. "I have to go now." She stood up but Lucy made no move to see her out. Hannah realised that she'd fallen asleep where she was sitting, head on the table and crept out of the flat, another missing child – now adult – to add to her portfolio.

CHAPTER TWELVE

The box of Judy's things Hannah had taken from Paul's flat was in her office. She had had them taken from her when the police assumed she had removed the items from Judy's flat. Now the box was sealed – with a short printed note from Hannah inside – ready to be delivered to "that woman" as Hannah thought of her. She was tempted not to bother then she hoped that Judy would be embarrassed that Hannah had been through Paul's flat and found her personal items. Or perhaps that was assuming too much sensitivity on Judy's part. Brazen bitch.

Hannah was still furious at being arrested in Judy's home. The woman was without doubt one of the nastiest cows she'd ever come across. And now she was no nearer knowing about Judy's forthcoming book. She prayed fervently that someone would take an injunction out.

Maybe she should contact the solicitor at *The News*? She dialled his number but it was busy so she wrote a note to herself to call later. Her mind seemed a bit foggy which was, she assumed, caused by all the stress of the previous months and the worry about Tom. So writing things down became second nature.

On impulse she rang Neville Rogers, Paul's solicitor. He answered immediately and seemed pleased to hear from her.

After the social pleasantries, Hannah got to the point. "Neville do you know anything about this book Judy

Barton has written?"

Neville was silent for a moment as though considering what his answer should be. "Yes I do as a matter of fact. I had a call from Larry Jefferson at *The News* and I asked the publishers for a set of proofs. As a trustee of Paul's estate, I told them I was acting on behalf of his daughter."

Hannah was really glad Elizabeth had someone else acting in her best interests and that Neville took his role as trustee so seriously. "Thank you. And what do you think?"

"Well it won't win the Booker that's for sure... Sorry," he said into the silence, which followed that remark, "I was being facetious."

"I seem to have lost my sense of humour since she had me arrested."

"What?"

Hannah explained what had happened.

"For heaven's sake, Hannah, why didn't you call me?"

"Should I have?"

"Yes!" He sounded exasperated. "I am a solicitor and you might have needed one if DS Benton hadn't turned up." He paused. "I'm glad her little publicity stunt backfired but she definitely has her eye to the main chance so be careful."

"And the book?"

"It's written as a love story. Fairly racy. I have been through it with a blue pencil and my wife is also reading it as she works in publishing. Obviously Judy has cast herself as the investigative journalist who saves the day etc etc... But apart from the themes of a few corrupt officials there's not much to link it to reality. And let's face it she doesn't know the half of it."

Hannah wondered if she had been worrying for nothing.

"The real problem," Neville continued, "is how they are publicising the book. Ms Barton is being presented as a journalist who investigated the ring which was importing the girls from Somalia..."

"What!"

"They are not saying so explicitly but the implication is there and that's what I'm working on. I understand Lord Gyles is taking this as a personal affront though God knows why."

"I could hazard a guess," Hannah said but didn't elucidate. "But thank you Neville. It's good to know you have our backs covered."

Neville made an odd sound. "And how are you apart from all this upset?"

"I'm fine. Just a bit tired but I think that's all the stress." She was tempted to tell him about the attack in St John's but she didn't want to sound needy, silly.

"Well take care and I'll keep you posted about Ms Barton's book."

When Hannah replaced the receiver she felt less panicky and decided to get rid of Judy's things there and then. She rang for a courier and was glad to see the back of the box when he arrived. What Judy would make of it all she didn't know and didn't care.

Hannah turned her attention to her romantic couple copy. A final read through and she'd email it to the features desk. It seemed such an irony to be writing about someone else's love story, while Judy was creating her own fiction and she herself felt out in the cold.

CHAPTER THIRTEEN

She was wide-awake now. The first spasm pierced through her abdomen like an arrow of fire. Now the pain seared through her. Wave after wave after wave. Her breathing was shallow. Each inhalation seemed to make it worse. She rolled over onto her side, edged herself off the bed and staggered to the bathroom. Blood was smeared down the inside of her thighs and she cried out as another spasm caught her as she lowered herself on to the loo and sobbed.

Her skin felt clammy. Eventually she eased herself off the toilet and stripped off her nightdress. Gingerly she stepped into the bath and stood under the shower watching the blood dilute then find its way down the plughole. When the water ran clear she turned off the shower, stepped out of the bath and wrapped herself in a towel. She found some sanitary pads in the bathroom vanity unit. Slowly she made her way back to her bedroom, retrieved some pants from a drawer and stuck a couple of pads inside. There were some painkillers in her bedside table drawer; she took two then placed the towel over the bloodstained sheet and eased herself onto the bed. She tried breathing slowly and deeply, waiting for the pills to take effect.

She must have dozed because she was jolted awake by another spasm and bit into the pillow to stop herself crying out. She took some more painkillers then went to the bathroom to change the pads now saturated in blood and clots. As she stared down on the mess that had been a fetus, she wept for what might have been. The worst thing was that she couldn't tell the one person who should have been there for her.

Exhaustion rendered her eyes so dry that the inside of her eyelids felt like sandpaper when she blinked. She needed to pull herself out of this but the lethargy was all consuming. Only Elizabeth had the power to energise her but that was in small bursts. Aware of Janet's concerned expression, Hannah made a show of going into her office to work. In reality, she sat in the armchair and stared into space. It had been an early miscarriage. More like a heavy period but that didn't make her feel any better. The loss seemed a metaphor for her relationship with Tom.

"Christ, Hannah, you should have called me." Linda poured some coffee as they sat at the kitchen table a few days later.

"And that would have achieved what exactly?" Hannah felt raw and irritable. "Sorry I didn't mean that. There was nothing anyone could do. You're the only person I've told."

Linda looked as though she wanted to ask about Tom but refrained. She sipped her coffee.

"I miscarried before I had Joel."

"And you never told me."

"I'm telling you now."

Hannah stared out of Linda's kitchen window. Watching Dave playing with the children in the garden, she wondered if Elizabeth would feel she was missing out when she was older and understood there was no father at home.

"I'm not sure what's worse." Linda broke the silence. "Losing a baby when you don't have children and there's the possibility that you never will or miscarrying when you know the joy of having a child? Either way there's pain and grief that has to be worked through."

"Maybe it was for the best." Hannah's voice was quiet and resigned.

Linda waited to see if Hannah would share her reasoning.

"I don't think I could cope with single parenting two children."

Again Linda wanted to ask about Tom. That elephant in the room seemed to fill the space between them. But she sensed Hannah's reserve. Whatever had happened during their holiday together, her friend obviously couldn't or wouldn't discuss it.

"Did you see the GP?"

"No." She could see Linda was about to scold her. "He was so dismissive when I phoned the surgery that I arranged an appointment at the Family Planning Clinic. Everything was okay."

"Good." Linda poured some more coffee and passed her a slice of cake. "So how are you feeling now?"

Hannah shrugged. "Tired. Emotional."

"It will get easier." Linda's hand was warm and comforting over hers.

Hannah smiled. "I know. It's just..." Whatever she was about to say was cut short by a scream from the garden. They both dashed outside to discover that Joel had banged into a corner of the house and a huge lump was forming on his forehead. Elizabeth was trying to comfort him to no avail and Dave was nowhere to be seen.

"Sorry. Sorry." Dave emerged from the house via the French windows. "I was changing Charlotte's nappy."

Linda picked up her son and kissed his bruise. Elizabeth toddled over to her mother and put her arms up for a cuddle too. Hannah could feel herself about to cry again and hid her face in her daughter's neck.

"Mama face wet."

Hannah sniffed and laughed as she brushed away the tears. Dave was staring at her but, unusually for him, said nothing.

"Come along young lady, time to go home." Hannah walked through the house to the hall where she'd left the buggy and strapped Elizabeth in.

Linda hugged her. "Take care," she mumbled into her hair. "And call if you need me."

"Thanks. If I don't see you before, we'll catch up after your holiday. Have a lovely time."

Linda pulled a face. "A fortnight with Dave's parents in their caravan in Wales. How I long for a Greek Island..." Her expression changed as she realised her blunder. "We'll have a lovely time."

As Hannah made her way home, she thought, not for the first time, how much she envied Dave and Linda but knew her life would never be like theirs. To her ears two weeks in a caravan in Wales sounded idyllic. But first France and a visit to her parents beckoned.

CHAPTER FOURTEEN

"Any news on the dead Aussie in Dulwich, Guv?" Mike Benton asked DI Turner as she passed his desk.

"Not yet. Still waiting for any info from Australia."

"Well let's hope it's not too long or Ms Weybridge will be finding a way to make it front page news."

"Let's hope not. Although a bit of publicity might help in uncovering who he really was." She paused looking over at the whiteboard. "What prompted that question?"

"You're not going to like this." Benton opened a file on his desk.

Claudia read his expression. "Bring it into my office sergeant and we can have a decent cup of coffee."

Mike followed the DI into her office and sat down while she made some filter coffee. She had even bought a mini fridge for her office to keep milk in. Class, Mike thought, and let his mind wander to the sort of office he'd set up once he had his promotion.

"So what won't I like?" Claudia placed his coffee on the desk.

"I found another one."

"Another what?"

"Another dead Australian. Four days before the Dulwich Library one."

"Where?" Claudia's voice was quietly controlled, always a sign she was furious.

Mike consulted the file. "Burgess Park. Francis Jones was found sitting under a tree by a group of kids. They thought he was asleep..."

"Shit. So why weren't we alerted?"

"Thought it was a natural. Local nick was trying to trace relatives. Eventually someone he had been supposed to be meeting contacted the station ... It doesn't look as though they did much more than put two and two together. Apparently the man he was meant to have met is an English relative. His details are here."

Claudia sat very still. "Right let's try a bit of damage limitation. Go and see the investigating officer and find out all you can. Take one of the DCs with you. I'll go and see this man, the relative. Any uniform you recommend to come with me?"

"PC Sheridan James. She was good with Lucy Peters and she's bright."

Claudia smiled and nodded. Mike left the room as she picked up the phone. Two dead Australian men. She sincerely hoped they didn't find anything to link them. The last thing they needed was a serial killer on their hands.

"To be honest, I'd been expecting him for some time." The man was in his forties, smartly dressed and welcoming when he answered the door to them. DI Turner and Sheridan James introduced themselves and they had been shown into a narrow sitting room, which ran the length of the house, with French windows opening on to a compact garden.

"What makes you say that, Mr Grayton?" Claudia's critical gaze took in the piles of books that seemed to be taking over the room.

Norman Grayton chuckled at the expression on the

DI's face. "I've been clearing out my father's house. He died recently and I couldn't bear to part with his books." He straightened the cuff on his shirt. "I'm a freelance editor and ..." he correctly interpreted Claudia's expression. "However back to the reason for your visit. Before he died my father told me and my brother that we had a half-brother. My mother had given birth to him before she met our father and he had been placed in some sort of orphanage." Norman Grayton focused on something he could see outside in the garden.

"Life was very different then. Especially for a young unmarried girl who found herself pregnant." Again he paused. "My father explained that my mother had 'confessed' everything to him and after their marriage they went to the orphanage to collect her son. But he wasn't there. The people in charge claimed he'd died. My father asked to see the death certificate and demanded to know why his wife hadn't been informed. As you can imagine it was a fraught and emotional confrontation."

Norman Grayton paused. "Are you sure I can't get you some tea, Inspector?"

"Would you like some, Mr Grayton? I could make it while you talk to DI Turner," Sheridan James offered.

"Thank you, dear, that would be nice. The kitchen is just through there–" he pointed to another door – "and everything is set out on the counter." He turned his attention back to Claudia Turner.

"In the end the orphanage managers owned up to the fact that my half-brother had been sent out to a better life in Australia and there was little anyone could do about it as he'd been adopted by a family over there."

"So you were expecting him because...?" Claudia Turner briefly wondered what Hannah would make of this story. Should she tell her?

"I'd heard of other Australians coming back to the UK to find their birth families. I hoped my brother would be one of them." His eyes filled with tears. "Maybe the travel and stress of searching for us had been too much for his heart."

Claudia smiled in relief when Sheridan came in with a tray of tea. Norman Grayton sipped his gratefully.

"I'm afraid, Mr Grayton, your brother may not have died of natural causes. It's early days in our investigations but another Australian man died in Dulwich library a few days after your brother. Their deaths may be connected."

Sheridan's speedy reaction meant she was just in time to take the mug before Mr Grayton dropped it. "But why? Why would anyone want them dead?"

"Thanks for your help in there," Claudia said as she attached her seat belt and Sheridan started the car. "I'm not great on emotional outpourings."

"My pleasure, Ma'am." PC James kept her thoughts to herself. She'd heard DS Benton referring to her as the Ice Queen. Sheridan didn't care. She was a good role model for women officers and one she was determined to emulate.

"Back to the nick?" Claudia nodded; her thoughts were on another continent.

DS Benton was back at his desk and at a nod from Claudia followed her and PC James into her office.

"So what do we have?"

"Local police thought it was a natural. They put out a small item in the local press. Then Mr Grayton got in touch with them. I've arranged for another PM just in case."

"Yes a good thing the brother hadn't gone ahead with a funeral but was trying to discover if there was any family in Australia. He didn't have much to go on but did find out that Francis Jones was divorced but had no children."

"In the kitchen there was a cuttings book." Both the DI and Benton focused on James. "I took a peek and Mr Grayton had obviously been looking into the Child Migration Scheme."

"And?"

"There was a PostIt on one page –" Sheridan opened her notebook. "On it was written: '?? contact newspapers ?? Hannah Weybridge??'" Sheridan raised her head, her face flushed.

Turner smiled. "Well spotted. I wonder if he has made contact with Hannah? Anything on that print, Mike?"

He shook his head. But it was beginning to look like Hannah had been targeted but by whom and for what purposes remained a mystery.

CHAPTER FIFTEEN

"It's me Lucy." The voice was a giveaway; Hannah didn't need the introduction.

"Hello Lucy. How are you?"

"Up a fucking gum tree."

"Oh? Why?" Hannah felt a moment of irritation. There were times when she could do without other people's problems. She took a deep breath and doodled on her notepad as she waited for Lucy's explanation.

"They've released Harry."

For a moment Hannah hadn't a clue what she was talking about. Then she realised that Lucy must mean that the police had released Harry's body for burial.

"And?"

"And how do I arrange his fucking funeral?"

Hannah's heart sank. "Didn't they give you a leaflet and some contacts?"

"Yes and the body is at the funeral place. You know ..."

"The chapel of rest."

"Yeah that." Lucy said nothing more. Hannah knew what was wanted of her. Death and funerals had become so much a part of her life.

"Okay Lucy, would you like me to go with you to sort it out?"

"Oh would you love? That's so kind."

Yes, thought Hannah, too bloody kind. Then she admonished herself for being a cow and arranged a time to meet Lucy.

•

They came out of the undertakers and stood for a moment in the warm summer drizzle. The weather reflected Hannah's mood. Her own grief was still raw and she hadn't heard anything from or about Judy Barton and her book.

"Fancy a drink?"

Hannah was about to refuse but the mute plea in Lucy's eyes made her change her mind. She forced her lips into a smile. "I think we both deserve one, don't you?"

Lucy sighed. "Let's go over there –" she pointed to The Horseferry Pub – "and I can see about having some drinks and sandwiches after the funeral. Good thing Harry had an insurance policy to cover his funeral. Bloody lot of money if you ask me."

Hannah agreed. She'd steered Lucy to the cheapest options but even so the costs added up. She wondered how expensive Paul's funeral had been. Neville Rogers had arranged it all. Now seeing what Lucy had gone through she was even more grateful to him.

The pub seemed crowded for the time of day to Hannah and she noticed that quite a few of the drinkers seemed to know Lucy and spoke to her as she made her way to the bar.

"You look a bit peaky." Lucy placed the gin and tonic in front of Hannah who had been miles away.

"Had an infection and it's left me a bit washed out."

"Well you want to look after yourself, my girl."

Hannah smiled but she was bored – with herself

mainly. She hated the way she was feeling but didn't have the energy to pull herself out of it. She glanced at her watch. "Have to be getting back to Elizabeth soon."

Lucy nodded. "Thanks for your help over there." Lucy hesitated. "Don't suppose you've found out anything about Edward, have you?"

Hannah sipped her drink. "Not yet, sorry." She saw the glimmer of joy in Lucy's eyes and wished she could offer some hope. "You have to reconcile yourself to the fact that we may never find him."

"I know. It's just... What the...?"

Hannah – face deathly white – had half-risen. Momentarily she seemed suspended before descending to her seat. She turned to Lucy. "Did you see him?"

"Who?"

Hannah's face was ashen. "Sorry Lucy. I've got to go." And with that she picked up her bag and made for the door. But Tom had disappeared.

Hannah had hailed a black cab on York Road. She was exhausted and could only think about getting home and being able to relax. No sooner had she got into her office than the telephone rang. She considered letting it go through to answerphone then picked up the receiver.

"Hello Hannah, I've found some old letters and documents that I thought you might like to see." Sheila's voice sounded conspiratorial on the phone. "Don't mention it to Janet, though."

"Okay. Is there a reason not to tell her?"

"I don't want to worry her."

Hannah wondered if this was just an elaborate ruse to

get her to visit. If so she'd have to be careful. Janet had mentioned that her mother could be manipulative and she didn't want to find herself at the woman's beck and call. She'd had enough of that with Lucy.

"When would be a good time for you, Sheila? I have to be at the newspaper offices for the next few days. How would early next week suit you?"

There was a momentary silence. Possibly Sheila was weighing up her options. "Or you could give Janet a sealed package for me and not tell her what was inside?"

"No early next week's fine. Afternoons suit me better."

Somehow she got through the rest of the afternoon and evening. A bath and an early night beckoned. However sleep didn't come easily. Her thoughts were too intrusive. She had considered leaving a message for Tom at the number he'd given her but if it was him she'd seen in the pub there seemed little point. Had he spotted her and then left?

Maybe it wasn't him at all. She remembered the time she had thought she'd seen Paul in the Pen and Ink pub. She felt an icy grip around her heart. It was soon after that she'd learned that Paul had committed suicide while on remand. Of course, as she now knew, he hadn't killed himself but he was dead.

Dear God don't let Tom be dead. Not after everything they'd been through. She had tasted despair before and thought she wouldn't have to again. It would be just too ... convenient was the word which jumped into her mind and she wondered. Convenient for whom? The middle of the night was not conducive to coherent thought. She turned the pillow over and tried the breathing exercise the therapist had given her.

And there it was, the smell of freesia again. What did it mean? The scent enveloped her and she could feel her muscles relax and a smile played at her lips as she sank into oblivion.

CHAPTER SIXTEEN

"God you look awful!" DI Claudia Turner didn't mince her words as she followed Hannah into the sitting room. She'd phoned in the afternoon to see if Hannah would be in and free for a visit. They hadn't seen each other since Hannah's holiday with Tom and the DI was shocked by Hannah's appearance.

"Thanks for that boost to my self-esteem." Hannah hadn't bothered to change for Claudia's visit. She was wearing a grey baggy tracksuit the colour and fit of which matched her mood. Claudia, of course, looked amazing in a cotton frock and jacket. Nothing like her usual smart work suits.

"Sorry, it's just I've seen you at your worst and frankly …" Claudia had always admired what she saw as Hannah's fragility balanced by her strength. The scales had obviously tipped – in the wrong direction.

Hannah didn't let her finish. "I've had an infection and a bad period hasn't helped." Describing her miscarriage as a "bad period" seemed like sacrilege. The bleeding and the physical pain were over now. But not the anguish and sense of loss she felt for what might have been. The grief that stalked her. Her practical, logical side knew that a baby at this stage of her life would be disastrous. She certainly didn't want to put Tom in a position of having to become a father in his state. And she couldn't do it on her own. Not again. On the other hand this might have been her last chance for another baby. With a concentrated effort she brought herself back to the present.

"No, I don't suppose it has." Whatever else Claudia thought she kept to herself and Hannah was glad of her discretion. "Are you okay with wine or are you on medication?" The DI produced a bottle of Chablis from her bag. "Nicely chilled."

"No I'm not." Hannah managed a smile. "On medication that is. And you've brought my favourite wine so you must be after something." She went out to the kitchen and returned with two glasses and a corkscrew. Claudia did the honours.

"So apart from the infection and menstrual problems, how are you?" Claudia raised her glass and drank some wine.

Hannah sipped hers. "I'll survive."

"Good. I was wondering if you should do some self-defence classes given your predilection for finding yourself in tight corners..."

Hannah stared at her. Then laughed. "I've been beaten up and threatened by a pimp, had a gun pointed at me and my child, been abducted, assaulted by a gang." Hannah shook her head. "Yes maybe I should."

Claudia opened her bag and retrieved a leaflet, which she passed to Hannah. "These are the courses the police run. I could get you on one whenever you feel ready?" Claudia didn't mention what had happened at St John's. She'd wait to see if Hannah would.

Hannah glanced at the image of a woman throwing a man. "Thanks I'll let you know. Although I hope I won't need those skills in the future."

It was Claudia's turn to laugh. "You've turned over a new leaf then?"

"I don't go looking for trouble you know." Hannah sounded irritated.

Claudia seemed to consider this. "I hear you're helping Lucy Peters with the arrangements for her brother's funeral and going through some personal papers."

Hannah nearly spat her wine. "Well get to the point why don't you? Goodness, Claudia how on earth do you know that and more importantly why are you interested?"

"Off the record?" Hannah nodded. "There was something suspicious about her brother Harry's death." Claudia inspected one of Elizabeth's books, which was lying on the table. For a moment *Each Peach Pear Plum* seemed to absorb her attention. "Something was lodged in his throat."

"So he choked to death. People do." Hannah knew she sounded hard. She needed to get life back into perspective.

"Post mortem, we think."

"What was it?" Hannah felt nauseous.

"Sorry can't share that with you at the moment but it was strange – and it could have been personal."

Hannah looked perplexed. "You don't think Lucy had anything to do with it, do you?"

"Not ruling anything out, Hannah. I'm keeping an open mind."

"Well you're taking your time."

"Better to be thorough and not jump to conclusions."

"So presumably you know how long he'd been dead."

"Yes and it doesn't tally with what the neighbour said. He definitely hadn't been out to collect his pension the previous week."

"Does Lucy know she's a possible suspect?"

"Not sure really. The solicitor Simon Ryan provided has been kept in the loop. Strange that?" She sipped her wine.

"What?"

"That she contacted an eminent QC and he responded the way he did. Still he was her second choice. You were her first." For a moment Hannah wondered what it would be like to have Claudia as her boss. In many ways she was like the editor at *The News*. Driven. Calculating...

"So I hear." Hannah was still cross with her mother for not taking the message properly. Not that it would have made any difference, as she wouldn't have been able to be there for Lucy. "But regarding Simon Ryan, Lucy seemed close to his brother, Father Patrick, and maybe that's why."

The mention of the priest who was killed in St Thomas's hospital while supposedly being protected by the police led both women's thoughts off in different directions. Neither spoke for a few moments. Then Claudia poured some more wine.

"Have you heard from Tom?"

"No, but I don't expect to for a while. Have you heard anything?" At least on this subject she didn't need to hide anything from Claudia. She assumed the DI had been informed of Tom's rehab or had found out about it. She thought about mentioning seeing him in the pub with Lucy but decided Claudia might think she was going crazy.

Claudia shook her head. "Above my pay scale. High security and all that. I hope he gets through this…"

"Yes. So do I."

Claudia looked as though she wanted to say something then changed her mind. "Any interesting stories you're working on that are going to test me?"

Hannah smiled. "Nothing unless you're interested in the winners of The UK's Most Romantic Couple?"

Claudia snorted. "Have you gone back to women's mags?"

"It feels like it sometimes. But no it's for *The News* who are trying to keep me gainfully employed and out of harm's way."

"Good for them." Claudia poured the last of the wine into their glasses. "So have you found anything interesting in Lucy's brother's papers?"

"I'd have thought your team would have been through them?"

"To be honest I don't think anyone did. Uniform who answered the call to the flat thought it was a natural death. It was only later that the post mortem revealed… and perhaps the papers were hidden away and Lucy knew where to find them."

"You seem to have a bit of a downer on Lucy."

"No not really just hate loose ends." Claudia smiled.

"So can I ask you something?"

"You can ask…" Claudia's expression made Hannah think she wouldn't want to be interrogated by her.

"Do you know anything about the man who was found dead in Dulwich library?" Hannah remembered the librarian's description of him as looking haunted.

Nathalie had also remarked on his tan. But lots of people had bronzed this summer...

Now it was Claudia's turn to almost choke on her drink. "Good lord wasn't a body in Peckham Pond enough for you?" She was referring to the last case they'd both been involved in which had led them to a criminal group responsible for young Asian girls going missing and "honour" killings.

"Oh you know me – can't keep my inquisitive journo's nose out of things."

"Ye-es. Well I can tell you we've drawn a blank there. Odd though."

"What's odd?"

"The chief librarian there gave us some papers he'd asked her to photocopy." Hannah could feel the hairs on the back of her neck tingling. "But we couldn't make head nor tail of them. We're in the process of trying to contact his family in Australia but it's proving difficult. He doesn't seem to have married or have living relatives there. Apparently he'd been an orphan brought up in some sort of religious institution that doesn't exist any more. By all accounts he was researching his family in London." She eyed Hannah thoughtfully. "About as much as you already know I assume?"

Hannah saw no reason to prevaricate. "Yes it's odd though as you say."

"Not a great story for *The News*, I assume?"

Hannah laughed. "You never know." She wondered if she should confide in Claudia what she'd learned about the children who went missing after the war and the Child Migration Scheme.

"But if there had been another suspicious death?"

Hannah stared at her. "Has there been?"

"Four days before the Dulwich death, an Australian man was found dead in Burgess Park."

"But..?"

"Some kids found him sitting under a tree. Appeared like a natural death at the time. But DS Benton made the link." Claudia refilled their glasses. "You haven't been contacted by a Norman Grayton then?"

"No, why?"

"He's the half-brother of the Burgess Park victim, Francis Jones. When we visited him, an eagle-eyed constable saw a file he had and that he'd written a note with your name on. He's been researching the scheme sending British children to Australia after the war."

Hannah pulled a face. "News to me and I won't hold my breath – my contract's coming up for renewal so we'll see."

"Are you thinking of moving on?"

"I really don't know. The contract does give me financial security and I've got used to that. Better the devil you know and all that. Plus the editor and owner have been good to me and they've protected me. I'd feel vulnerable without them. But sometimes I feel trapped." For a moment Hannah struggled to keep the tears at bay.

Claudia leaned forward and placed her hand over Hannah's. "You do have other friends you know." There was an emphasis on the way Claudia said friends. She wasn't sure she wanted friends in high places like that. It was a highly placed person who had tried to manipulate, bully and threaten her and her daughter during her last investigation. And had nearly succeeded.

"It's good to have your friendship anyway." They looked at each other recognising the distance they'd come and that, in fact, they were friends. Of sorts. Ill matched. But friends.

They finished their wine and Claudia left, having phoned for a minicab. As Hannah rinsed the glasses she thought about the inspector. There was something engaging about her despite her coolness. She enjoyed their chats over a bottle of wine and she guessed that sometimes Claudia felt as lonely as she did.

She drank a couple of glasses of water then went to bed wondering about what had been stuffed in Harry's throat and why Lucy might still be a suspect. It also occurred to her as she was slipping into sleep that Claudia hadn't mentioned the débarcle with Judy Barton. Perhaps Mike Benton hadn't told her. Nor about the incident in St John's. Who had she discovered there? And how did he know her. Those questions went round and round in her mind when she woke in the early hours but she was no nearer an answer.

CHAPTER SEVENTEEN

Who would want to kill a man from Australia who was researching his family history? Nathalie had said he looked haunted and she wondered what demons beset him. Claudia had said he'd been brought up in some sort of religious institution in Australia and didn't seem to have any family there. How sad. The photocopies that the librarian had given her meant nothing to her. Just a list of names. Some had dates by them. A question mark with a last known address next to it. But underlined several times was Blackwater House, in Wiltshire. She did a search through WebCrawler but found nothing.

She'd have to check through cuttings and microfiches and the best place to do that would be at *The News* offices. Well she'd have to face everyone at some time after the fiasco with Judy Barton. She sent an email to Rory: *Do you think it's okay for me to come in to do some research?* His reply came minutes later. *Of course. Be good to see you.*

Decision made she changed her dress and applied some make-up. The tan she'd acquired in Corfu made her appear healthier than she felt and for that she was grateful. She booked a minicab. Might as well make use of her account while she still could. Leaving a note for Janet who was at the toddler group with Elizabeth, she picked up her briefcase and left the house, carefully switching on the alarm and locking the door behind her. The car pulled up outside the house. She was relieved to see it wasn't one of her regular drivers who liked to chat about everything under the sun and got into the back seat and ran through her mind everything she had learned about the dead Australians – she now included Mr Grafton's half-brother, Francis Jones – and the missing children. She arrived at *The News* offices with more questions and few answers.

Hannah had already requested the cuttings department to search out anything they could find on Blackwater House but knew she'd have to refine her searches to make any sense of Jeff Collins's sparse notes.

On the desk she normally used, Hannah found a pile of envelopes, miscellaneous mugs with varying degrees of beverage left in them and old copies of newspapers and magazines. She dumped a pile of stuff on to the floor, found the internal envelope bearing her name that she was searching for, and emptied the contents onto the space she'd created. The information on Blackwater House was disappointingly meager but there was a note from the librarian: *Just an initial sweep. More to follow. Welcome back.*

Blackwater House – the very name held Dickensian connotations for her. There was a black and white photo of the building that looked as though it might once have been an imposing family residence. It was just outside a largish village, which apparently was now a small town in Wiltshire. A church was in view next to the house. Hannah counted the windows at the front and wondered how many children it had housed. Maybe there were dormitories. The photo made her feel uneasy though she couldn't have said why.

She leafed through the cuttings. Not much to go on. She'd have to check through the info held on the microfiches.

She'd have liked to talk it through with Rory but he had taken the afternoon off. It was strange to think of him having an existence outside of his role here.

"Hello Hannah, welcome back." The deputy editor paused at her desk and took in the unusual clutter. "Come and have a chat when you have a moment." And with that he was on his way.

Hannah went over to the news desk secretary. Jo smiled up at her. "What can I do you for?"

Hannah laughed. "Don't ask. But could you email me any meeting notes I've missed and editorial meeting dates?"

"Sure. Sorry about your desk. We've had some casuals in…"

Hannah glanced across to where she normally worked when she was in the office. "It's only a desk." For a moment she felt as though something had stared back at her. That feeling again… She was being fanciful but she imagined some evil stalking her. Totally preposterous, of course.

Hannah knocked on the door of the deputy editor's office. Terry Cornhill looked up and smiled. "Come in and shut the door behind you."

Hannah felt as though she'd been called into the headmaster's office. Terry was wearing one of his Fair Isle V-necked sweaters that made him look like an absent-minded professor but it was just a façade. He was a principled journalist who had a contacts book that apparently read like the A to Z of some of the most influential people in the country. Hannah had had reason to be grateful for his support and help in the past.

"Sorry about that last story about the most romantic couple winners. A freelance we had booked let us down at the last minute so…" He let the conclusion evaporate between them. "So how does it feel to be back in the saddle?"

"If you mean the dead Australian –" she was holding fire on Claudia's information that there were two dead Australians.

"I do. And word has it that there could be repercussions."

"Another can of worms then?"

"Yes. Have you been in touch with that social worker in Nottingham? She's done a lot for people affected by the Child Migration Scheme. Helped them to trace their families." He handed her a piece of paper with an email address and telephone number.

"Right."

"Keep me posted."

"Of course." Hannah stood up to leave.

"Try not to worry about Judy Barton and her book. It'll all sort itself out. You'll see." His phone rang. Hannah mouthed "thank you" and left the office.

"Hannah there was a call for you – from a Mr Norman Grayton. He left his number and asked if you would call him back." The secretary handed a piece of paper to her.

"Thanks. Did he say what it was about?"

"No but said he'd only talk to you."

Hannah went back to her desk. She stared at the number. It wouldn't hurt to call back and it was reassuring that he'd rung the office. As she dialled the number she remembered the name. Claudia had told her that he was the half-brother of the other dead Australian, the one found in Burgess Park. "Norman Grayton." The voice sounded gruff.

"Hello Mr Grayton, Hannah Weybridge returning your call." By the end of the conversation, she'd agreed to meet Norman Grayton. She rang DI Turner and left a message.

Hannah booked an account car straight to Kennington where Norman Grayton lived. Their telephone conversation had been brief with Hannah agreeing to visit him on her way home. When she arrived, Norman Grayton took a long time to answer the door. When he did he seemed flustered.

"I'm so sorry Hannah, I've just had a rather disturbing telephone call." He showed Hannah into the sitting room, which was tidy apart from the piles of books, bringing a smile to Hannah's face. She could imagine DI Turner's reaction. "My father's –" the sweep of his hand indicated the books. "He died a few months ago and I've been clearing his house. Can't bring myself to get rid of them. Please sit down."

Hannah sat in a leather chair that matched the sofa and looked down the length of the room to the garden beyond the open French windows. "What a lovely room. Have you lived here long?"

"Yes." Norman Grayton ran his hands down his light green chinos his expression sombre. "It seems so odd to be mourning someone I never met. But I do. It is such a tragic irony that he died just before we could meet. And now the police say he may have been murdered."

"It would seem that way."

Norman examined at his watch. "Would you like a drink? I have some wine in the fridge."

Hannah was struck by the way Norman's mind veered from one subject to another. "I'd love one." She thought of Elizabeth – she could still get home in time to give her a bath and read her a story. She'd forewarned Janet.

Norman returned with the wine. "I work from home," he said apropos of nothing. "I'd been expecting – hoping – that Francis would contact me after my father told me about how he had been shipped off to Australia. Poor child to have been told his mother had died and that he had no other relatives." He sipped the wine. "My mother was a very gregarious person. She loved her sons – my brother and me – and you would never have known her secret sorrow for the boy she lost. My father gave me this envelope." He handed it to Hannah.

The contents were sparse: a birth certificate, a couple of hazy black and white photos... And the address of the foster home she'd taken the little boy to. It was somewhere in Kent. Then she opened a folded sheet of paper: a typewritten letter stating that Francis had been transferred to Blackwater House in Wiltshire. No reason was given.

Hannah looked up. "I wonder why they transferred Francis?"

Norman shrugged. "To make it more difficult for her to visit him?"

That made sense. Especially as that seemed to be the place the children were sent off to Australia from, although there must have been other orphanages which participated in the scheme.

"Apparently she never mentioned the father." Norman took several gulps of wine.

There was the sound of a key in the lock and a voice calling, "Dad?"

Norman smiled. "In the sitting room, Charles." The person in question came in and did a double take seeing Hannah.

"Charles, this is Hannah Weybridge, a journalist." Norman's son was about twenty with floppy fair hair and an air of his father about him – albeit more untidy.

"Hi. Are you here about what happened to Francis?" He flopped down onto the sofa next to his father.

"Yes." Hannah looked questioningly at Norman.

"I'd be honoured if you would include Francis in your investigations, Hannah. These men deserve something better from us. From a country that cheated them out of their birthright and sold them like slaves."

Hannah was surprised by his outburst but could not have agreed more. She left shortly afterwards having promised to keep Norman – and his son – up to date with anything pertinent she discovered. On her way home she wondered about the "very disturbing phone call" which Francis hadn't mentioned again. Perhaps it was nothing to do with his dead brother. She hoped so.

CHAPTER EIGHTEEN

"Hi, Edith, isn't it? I'm a friend of Lucy's next door." She tried what she thought of as her most disarming smile to no effect. Hannah had timed her visit to coincide with a trip Lucy said she was making to visit a friend. She'd made it sound mysterious and Hannah wondered why. Still it served her purpose – she could visit the neighbour without Lucy knowing. At least beforehand.

The woman standing in front of her was wearing a long flowing skirt that could have been a match for Joseph's coat of many colours. Her orange t-shirt clashed her cropped purple hair. She looked unimpressed. "And?"

"I wondered if I could ask you a few questions about Harry."

"I've said all I have to say to the police. Ask them."

Why the belligerence? "I have spoken to them but I'm a journalist on *The News* doing some background research to another story I'm working on."

The woman stared at her. "Oh yes, and you're a friend of Lucy's are you? What's your name? Any ID?"

Hannah produced her NUJ card from her wallet. "Hannah Weybridge," the woman read out loud. She returned the card without a shadow of a smile. "Come in."

The layout of flat was the mirror image of Harry's – now Lucy's – but there the similarities ended. The hall was painted in a vivid yellow and, above the dado rail, was covered with artifacts and images all in startling hues. As Edith opened the sitting room door, Hannah was almost blinded by the riot of colours: two sofas one purple, one lime green were placed at right angles against the walls and were covered with an assortment of cushions in contrasting fabrics. The fireplace was pink and red with some leaves highlighted in orange and you could hardly see the colour of the walls for framed pictures of a vibrancy which made Hannah wish she hadn't taken off her sunglasses.

"I'm an artist," she said by way of explanation. "And I know who you are. You're the one who's been writing those exposés and nearly getting yourself killed in the process."

"That's one way of describing me, I suppose."

"Brave lady." Hannah didn't comment. Edith indicated one sofa and sat on the other, her clothes clashing with the riot of colour. "So what's so interesting about Harry?"

"You tell me. You had his spare key so he must have trusted you."

"After a fashion I suppose." Edith paused. "At least he didn't see me as a threat."

"Was he threatened then?" Hannah was intrigued. It hadn't occurred to her that Harry had felt threatened before his death.

Edith stared out of the window. "Did you see the place when Lucy moved in, before she got rid of things? Three television sets balanced on top of each other so that he could watch each channel and not miss anything?"

Hannah nodded.

"Before he retired, he worked in the print department

of one of the government offices. He always hinted that it involved secret papers. He was probably exaggerating, of course. People like to feel important however menial their task. But he was awarded the BEM. He was so proud of it, poor sod."

"And he told you all this."

Edith nodded. "Many times. Sometimes I'd see him in The Hope & Glory and we'd have a drink or walk back together. He was often sad."

"So how long had he lived here?"

"He was rehoused after his mother died." Hannah knew this of course. "That must have been four, five years ago. I moved here at about the same time. I used to live at my studio but it got a bit cramped. This –" she waved a hand at the walls – "is the overflow."

Hannah glanced round. It made her head spin. Then her eye caught an expensive camera on the coffee table, which was piled with books, newspapers and cuttings. "Are you a photographer too?"

"Sort of. I always have my camera ready for research. Although my art appears mostly abstract it is inspired by what I see around me."

Hannah considered this. "Do you take photos of the square and the people who live here?"

Edith didn't say anything for a moment then she got up. "Wait here, I'll show you something." She left the room and returned with a pile of contact sheets and larger prints. "The answer to your question is yes. I'm working on a project at the moment. These are all of residents or people who hang out here. Sometimes people turn up to do a bit of business."

Hannah's did her best to keep her face from betraying her excitement.

"Couple of hookers live here and some of the kids deal. Anyhow you can see life in all its glory here." She leafed through the photographic paper. "Here's Harry. He let me take one of him watching his three TV screens." Hannah leaned forward to study Lucy's twin.

"I imagine he'd have been quite attractive in his day. Gone to seed obviously but now and again you got a glimpse of what might have been or could have been. He was very secretive about his past. I wondered if he was gay – you know living with his mother all those years. But I don't think he was. However he was lonely. He'd go down the pub, talk football or whatever. But there was a deep sadness there. You can see it in this one." She passed another photo to Hannah. Two lost souls she thought as Lucy again came to mind.

"Have you taken any of Lucy?"

Edith gave her a strange look. "I took a lot down at Cardboard City. Here –" she passed an envelope. The first image was of Sherlock. It was a shock she managed to cover with a cough.

Edith either didn't notice or chose to ignore her reaction. "I have another set you may be interested in." She left the room again and Hannah leafed through the photos of homeless people looking relaxed, some smiling at the camera. Her breath caught in her throat as she recognised Father Patrick in one.

Edith came back with another envelope. "There's someone who met Harry on the corner of the square... and another different person here..."

Hannah took and examined the photos. "When was this?"

Edith took one of the photos and examined at the reverse that she had dated. "It was a week or so before he was found dead." Their eyes met. "So one of them could have been his killer." The silence between them was broken by the sound of a clock chiming the hour somewhere in the flat.

"Could I borrow these?" She caught Edith's expression of mistrust. "I could pay you for the loan. I don't want to publish any. At least not without your consent and a proper fee." Hannah took out her wallet. "I can offer £100 for the loan but I'll need a receipt."

Edith smiled and surprised Hannah by pulling out of her bag a book of receipts. "This do?" Hannah nodded and Edith put carbon paper between two pages and wrote: *Received with thanks. £100 for loan of six photos to be returned within fourteen days.* She tore out the page and handed it to Hannah. She glanced at her watch. "Sorry I've got to leave."

There was a loud crashing noise followed by several expletives. Edith smiled sadly. "My neighbour has returned."

Hannah looked horrified.

"Don't worry. It doesn't happen very often. I suppose she has to get used to living within walls again."

CHAPTER NINETEEN

Hannah phoned Sheila from her mobile and popped in to see her on her way home.

"I've been thinking a lot about our last conversation," she said as they went into the sitting room. "We were evacuated during the war but I was one of the lucky ones as my mum came with us. That meant we had lodgings that were okay and mum got some work on a farm. We went to the local school with other kids from our area." Sheila paused while Hannah poured their coffees and handed her a cup. "Mum hated it. We didn't understand, of course. It was an adventure for us. Like a holiday. Everyone, of course, had been issued with a gas mask in its own little box. As evacuees we were given a list of what we had to take with us. It wasn't a long list but some of the kids had never owned their own toothbrush. As I said we were the lucky ones. Some children were treated really badly and some kids were right little terrors. The thing was some children disappeared."

Hannah placed her mug onto the table slowly. "How do you mean 'disappeared'?" Sheila had mentioned her cousin on her previous visit. This was another development.

"Well I would have thought the meaning is obvious. They weren't there any more." Shelia frowned and Hannah wondered if it was pain that was making her grumpy. She paused to slice the cake holding the knife with both hands and pushed a plate towards Hannah.

Her swollen fingers were bent at an awkward angle as though they'd been broken and reassembled in the dark. Her nails, however, were beautifully manicured. Hannah wondered whose art that was. Janet's?

"Some of the children who were there, their mothers worked in munitions factories or were posties or whatever back in London. Some were killed in the blitz. I remember mum saying something like poor little blighters when kids were told their parent had died. Soon after they were sent to an orphanage. I remember my mum saying she didn't know why they just didn't let them stay with the families they had been placed with. But no one asked. Not then. It wasn't like now. We needed someone like you around then, Hannah."

Sheila was looking at her strangely and Hannah wasn't sure if she was being complimented or made fun of. It wasn't a comfortable feeling.

"So where was this orphanage or were there lots of them?"

"The one we knew about was Blackwater House."

Hannah had to remind herself to breathe. Coincidence or not?

"It was an old manor house but it had been taken over by the authorities. Think the church may have been involved as well. They usually are when things like that happen."

"Things like what?"

"What I said kids going missing. Handy churchyard for burials or so rumour had it."

"Children were murdered?"

"Couldn't say. Some said they were suicides. And

others just went missing but that was just when the war was over and they shipped kids over to Australia."

"But they were orphans presumably being sent to a better life."

"Who knows if it was a better life but I do know that some of them weren't orphans. Parents – like my aunt – turned up looking for their children. Not many got the answer they were searching for."

Hannah was silent. Was the man who had died in the library connected in some way to a post war evacuation of children to Australia? The Blackwater House link might suggest so.

"Well that's food for thought."

Sheila fished in the bag that was fixed to her Zimmer frame. "This is the letter I found. About my cousin."

Hannah removed the thin folded sheet of paper from the envelope addressed to a Mrs D. Waterman. She glanced over the contents. Then read the letter again slowly. The complete lack of empathy shown by the writer, some nameless civil servant, was devastating. She couldn't begin to imagine how a mother would feel on opening that envelope. On being told that her son had been transported to a country on the other side of the world, to a better life than his family could hope to give him. That the letter had been read countless times was evident by the wear on the fold.

"What a deeply shocking and offensive letter to receive. Your aunt must have been devastated."

"Yes. Of course I was only a child but I knew something awful had happened. She was never the same."

The telephone rang. Sheila manouevered herself in her

chair in order to reach out for the phone. Hannah saw her wince as she did so.

"Yes speaking." She glanced over at Hannah. "No I'm with someone at the moment... No ring me later." She gave no clue as to who her caller was but seemed eager for Hannah to leave.

"Let me know how you get on. Sorry, would you mind seeing yourself out?"

"Of course not. Take care." Hannah left the room and the flat wondering just why Sheila had got her there. Was she building up to asking her to investigate her cousin's disappearance? If so she was going a strange way about it. For someone who seemed nothing if not direct she was strangely reticent.

CHAPTER TWENTY

The following day they were in the kitchen drinking coffee chatting about Elizabeth's various activities when Janet cleared her throat and changed the subject. "You're looking better," she said tentatively, perhaps worried that her words would offend her employer.

Hannah smiled at her, only too aware that she had been difficult company. The veil of sorrow seemed to be lifting. A smaller ache. A lighter shade of grief.

"Thanks – sorry I've been such a misery of late."

Janet stared down at her hands. "You know, you can talk to me. I would never betray anything you say to me in private." Her cheeks were flushed.

"I do trust you, Janet. You take care of Elizabeth – for me that's testament to how much I value you." She paused uncertain whether to carry on then decided Janet had been through enough for her to be told. "I had a miscarriage." Janet said nothing. "An early miscarriage. I hadn't realised I was pregnant at first. It wasn't planned and … and then I lost it." She took a deep breath. "I'm sorry I didn't take you into my confidence."

Janet put her cup down; her face was flushed. "I thought you were pregnant and then when you didn't say anything I wondered if you …" Janet couldn't put that thought into words.

"No." Hannah sniffed noisily. "It just wasn't to be. I'm sorry I didn't share it with you. After everything you have done for me and Elizabeth."

"Oh I'm not suggesting I had a right to know."

"I understand that. Anyway I'm coming out of the fog now. It was a shock and I hated what was happening to me."

Janet smiled. "Thank you for telling me. I was worried that you were unhappy with my work or..."

"Not at all. I really appreciate the way you fit in with us. We've been through so much together."

Janet laughed. "That's true."

"Do you ever regret giving up your career?"

Janet stared at her. "I'm sorry?"

Hannah knew it was a now or never moment to be totally honest with each other. "Do you ever regret giving up your career in the police?"

Janet's face had flushed crimson. "Did Tom tell you?"

Hannah looked away. Another confession. "No he didn't actually. I saw a photo-frame turned face down in your home and, I'm afraid, I peeped. It was you in uniform."

Janet was silent for so long, Hannah thought she must have offended her beyond repair.

"Tom suggested this job to me. I was at my wits' end with trying to keep up with shifts and look after my mother. I had previously trained as a nanny before joining up so it made sense. I'm sorry I wasn't completely honest on my CV."

"I don't care about that." Hannah took a deep breath. "To be honest I am reassured by your police training and I have no complaints at all about your work. It's just that it must be rather tame for you after..." Hannah didn't complete her sentence as Janet burst out laughing.

"You must be joking."

Hannah laughed too. "I suppose I must be."

Elizabeth called out from upstairs having woken from her nap. "I'll pop into the study before she sees me," Hannah said. "I've got some work to do this afternoon."

As she dialed the number, Hannah stared out into her garden, listening to her daughter's chuckles as she splashed in the paddling pool. Janet appeared nearly as wet as Elizabeth.

"DI Turner."

"Oh hello Claudia, I expected to have to leave a message. It's Hannah."

Claudia's tone was warmer now she knew who was calling. "You've just caught me. And I'd be extremely grateful if you've solved the riddle of these dead Aussies on my patch."

"Afraid not." Hannah was tempted to ask if she knew that Janet was ex-job but decided that was unfair. "But I do have some interesting photos you might like to see."

"Of?"

"Harry the late lamented brother of Lucy."

Claudia was silent. "The neighbour took them and it seems like someone may have been tailing him before he died."

"And she didn't think to tell us because?"

"I honestly don't think she saw the relevance. It was only after a fairly long discussion with her that she showed them to me. Anyway I got our art department to work on them and thought I'd share them with you."

"Okay. I'd like DS Benton to see them as well. Are you free now? I could send a car to collect you."

Hannah considered her neighbours. Police cars arriving in the street made her more of a curiosity. "Don't worry I'll use our account cars. I'll be about half an hour if that suits you?"

When Hannah arrived, Mike Benton was already in the DI's office. Claudia had cleared the table by the window in anticipation. Out of her briefcase, Hannah produced the first envelope. "These are of Harry Peters. Some are inside his flat as you can see. These ones here were taken in the square and the pub he sometimes went to. According to Edith, the neighbour, he always drank with the same group of three men. However if you look closely, in each of the later photos there's a fifth man. He's made an effort to change his appearance each time. Sometimes he wears a hat. His hair changes colour so could be a wig. His clothes look like they've come from a charity shop. I didn't noticed when I was looking at them with Edith, but when I examined them under the lights at work I saw his ring. He's wearing it in each photo. I had the guys at *The News* blow up this image. It looks like some sort of religious motif – do you see?"

Claudia and Mike exchanged a glance. "It's not much to go on."

"Here he is in the square." The police officers duly looked at the photo.

Hannah looked from Claudia to Mike. "You think I'm grasping at straws, don't you?" Neither agreed or disagreed. "But look –" she opened the envelope that included photos of Lucy. "Here he is again and it looks like Lucy could be his next target."

CHAPTER TWENTY-ONE

Hannah had been expecting a call from Simon Ryan. He was in London and invited her to dinner. It was short notice for Janet but she managed to pop home to see to her mother and return in time for Hannah to leave.

"You look great – that colour suits you," Janet said as Hannah waited for her cab.

Hannah did a little curtsey. "Thank you. I don't suppose I'll be late." The car arrived and she left happy in the knowledge that Elizabeth was always safe in Janet's care.

"Hannah, how wonderful to see you." Simon Ryan stood up as Hannah arrived at the table the waiter had directed her to in the cocktail bar at Rules in Maiden Lane. She knew it was the oldest restaurant in London but had never been there. The setting of plush red seating and panelled walls covered in framed photographs and famous newspaper cartoons suited the barrister. She was surprised at the warmth of Simon's greeting and the bear hug he gave her. "You're looking well."

Hannah sat in the chair he pulled out for her. "You too." She smiled but he could see the shadow of sadness.

The waiter hovered. "What would you like to drink?"

"A Dry Martini, please."

Simon beamed. "Good choice – their signature cocktail." The waiter moved away. "I thought we could have a drink up here before eating downstairs." He took Hannah's hand. "Hannah, I wanted to thank you for all your work and I'd like this to be a celebration for my brother. Patrick loved coming here –" he saw her surprised expression – "as my guest of course. A vicar's stipend hardly allows for elegant dining. But that doesn't mean he couldn't enjoy it. He always used to say that Jesus believed in the concept of abundance and he wished he could give more to those who needed it, which of course he has done with his bequest to St John's."

Her drink arrived. "A toast to Patrick's memory." Hannah raised her glass and thought of all the other people who had died ... then shook herself into the present.

Anyone seeing them would have thought them a handsome couple: Simon with his distinguished air and Hannah wearing a red tailored dress that complemented her figure and colouring. Anyone watching them, like the man across the room, might have thought they were either old friends or even lovers. Hannah could feel those eyes boring into her and as she sipped her drink she scanned the room. There were a few well-known faces who enjoyed the privacy this bar offered. Hannah leaned towards Simon. "Don't look right away but do you know anyone here who might be interested in either of us?"

Simon selected an olive from the silver dish. He didn't turn round. "There's a man at the bar who came in after you. From the way he's positioned it's difficult to see his face." He looked at his watch. "We'll see what happens when we leave to go to the restaurant. Now," he said, "have you had any success going through Lucy's papers? She's not a suspect by the way."

"I never thought she was but I am surprised you have shown such an interest." Hannah hoped her smile detracted from any implied criticism. She need not have worried, as a QC, Simon was used to far worse.

"I met her before Patrick died. At one of his services. I didn't go to many but this particular time, I noticed her sitting to one side, mumbling to herself. Uncharitably I thought she was probably drunk or on drugs but she was actually reciting the Apostles' Creed repeatedly. Then she began rocking to and fro and tears were pouring down her face. Patrick went and sat with her for such a long time I left and went back to the vicarage. When he returned Patrick seemed drained but he wouldn't say anything. Priests' confidentiality and all that. But there was a story there and I thought you'd be the person to uncover it."

"Sometimes discoveries are not what they seem."

"Meaning?"

"There is something in Lucy's past which haunts her and I think it's more complicated than it appears on first glance. A woman who used to be a neighbour told me she had become a nun and Lucy said she went to live with nuns."

"Your table is ready for you Mr Ryan." The waiter had arrived soundlessly.

Simon smiled at Hannah as they both stood and walked across the room. The person Hannah had thought was watching them was deep in conversation with the barman and did not look their way.

The restaurant was full and there was a buzz of excitement that a high level politician was dining with a top PR man and a famous actor was drawing attention to himself by speaking too loudly and laughing uproariously at everything the very young woman beside him said.

At their table they took a few minutes to check the menu before ordering. Simon chose some wine, which arrived promptly and when both had full glasses, he sat back in his seat. "To friendship." Hannah was about to reply when he continued, "And to Lucy may she survive her demons religious or otherwise."

Hannah couldn't think of a rejoinder so changed the subject. "Have you seen all the news about Aussie men coming over to find their families and dying?"

"Well I've read your pieces. I see DI Turner is investigating. You two seem to have hit it off. You make an interesting team."

Hannah looked surprised. "Well I wouldn't describe us as a team – and nor would she. When I first met her she was so hostile but we have become friends of sorts."

"And Tom?"

Hannah was grateful for the distraction of the arrival of their first course.

Simon said nothing. Waiting.

"Tom is in some sort of rehab unit. I don't know where and we're not in touch."

Her tone gave Simon his cue and he changed the subject to Elizabeth. "She must be a real joy. Something I would have liked to have had."

"What? Joy?"

"No, children."

Hannah laughed. "Not too late. Men don't have the

same biological clock ticking away."

Simon's expression was wistful as their main course arrived. "Well we can't all have everything we'd like in life."

"That's true. But tell me how have you managed to avoid being snapped up? I'd have thought you are eminently eligible."

Simon chuckled. "My brother and I are cut from the same cloth."

Hannah hadn't got a clue what he was alluding to and then the penny dropped and she felt her colour rise. How stupid of her. "I'm sorry I didn't mean to pry."

"I know you didn't. And not many people know so I'd prefer...

"Of course, I may be a journalist but I'm not a gossip."

Suddenly that struck them both as hilarious.

"How reassuring," Simon said then sotto voce "but not that our mystery man from the bar is dining with someone who is far from a stranger to me."

They had finished their main course.

"Go to the ladies. There's an exit there and I'll meet you outside." Fortunately Hannah wasn't wearing a jacket so she picked up her bag and did as she was told. Simon called over the waiter and turned his body so that no one could see their exchange. He handed cash over. "This should cover the bill and the two brandies I'd like you to bring to the table. Here's another £5 for your trouble and please help yourself to the drinks after a suitable time has passed."

The waiter nodded, discreetly pocketed the notes and went back to the bar. When he returned with the brandies, Simon had left.

Out in the street Simon guided her into Lumley Court, an alleyway that led down to The Strand. He hailed a taxi and opened the door for her. "Sorry Hannah I'll explain later." He handed her some notes for the fare. "Good thing a client just paid me in cash." He kissed his fingertips and extended them to her. "Speak soon." He slammed the door.

"Where to miss?" Hannah gave her address and sat back in the seat. Who on earth was Simon Ryan running from? And more importantly why?

CHAPTER TWENTY-TWO

"We seem to be behind with the returned books. Could you see to that, please Stacey."

The girl peered up from the magazine she was leafing through and Nathalie sighed – audibly. "You're here to work, you know, not catch up on the celebrity gossip."

When Stacey smiled, the sullen expression she usually wore disappeared, and she looked all of twelve rather than the sixteen-year-old who was waiting for her GCSE results. "Okay." She sashayed over to the wheeled shelving and began the task.

Nathalie carried on with some indexing in the reference section when the thud of a book being dropped followed by an expletive made her pause.

Stacey was on her hands and knees on the floor gathering some photos and pieces of paper. "Look what fell out of this book, Nathalie." She handed over her collection. "How long d'you think they've been in there then?"

"Not as long as you might think. Pass me that book would you?"

Great Expectations was delivered to her outstretched hand. Nathalie smiled at the ironic choice of book. The photos were old and frayed. There was part of a letter written in faded ink. What appeared to be a certificate. "Thank you Stacey. Could you just check through the other books there to see if there are any more treasures?"

"Cool." The girl seemed happier than the librarian

had ever seen her. She was humming something under her breath. Nathalie nearly laughed out loud when she realised it was the theme tune from "Between the Lines", one of her own favourite TV series.

Nathalie laid out the cuttings and photos carefully onto sheets of paper. Questions ran through her mind. Why? What for? The police had not come back to them about the death of the Australian man, Jeff Collins. She decided to ring them. In the end she had to leave a message, as no one was available to speak to her. She tried another number.

"Hello Hannah. Nathalie Vine here."

"Oh hello. You're a pleasant surprise. How are you?"

"Fine. Look I know this is daft but we've found some documents which I think may have been hidden in books by our dead Australian."

Hannah remained silent.

"I know it sounds far-fetched." She paused. "Do you have time to pop up to the library to have a look? I've rung the police and am waiting for them to get back to me."

Another pause. "Okay. I'll be with you as soon as I can."

As Nathalie replaced the receiver, Stacey said, "I wonder what happened to that other Australian?"

"What other Australian?"

"The one who turned up the day before the other one died. You must have seen him in here. He was quite tall. Pale for an Aussie, I thought."

Nathalie shook her head. "I don't remember another Australian. But unless I'd spoken to him, I don't suppose

I would have known where he came from. Did you speak to him?"

"Yeah once he asked me where the books on local history are. But he didn't go there, he picked up a newspaper and started reading it. He came in when the other guy was here. I thought they might be friends."

"Because..?"

"Because they came from the same country."

"Continent. Australia is a continent and it would be rather a coincidence if they did come from the same place."

Stacey shrugged.

"Did you tell the police this?"

"No I wasn't here on that morning, d'you remember? I was at the dentist."

Nathalie nodded. "So you were. Lucky escape for you."

"Missed all the excitement, you mean."

"Stacey, that's a dreadful thing to say."

The girl studied her nails. "But true."

"Well you can tell Hannah when she gets here."

"Tell me what?" the person in question asked having just arrived slightly out of breath in the upstairs reference room.

Nathalie was just about to repeat what Stacey had told her and then saw the young girl's face obviously eager to talk to a journalist from a national newspaper. "It's funny," the girl concluded, "but I thought he might have been putting on the accent a bit. We did accents and dialects in drama and he reminded me of an actor who had been coached in the accent."

"Seems odd," Hannah agreed when the girl had finished her tale. "And you haven't seen him since?"

Stacey shook her head.

"What did he look like – can you remember?"

"Just old and tanned really."

Nathalie laughed. "Remember Hannah to Stacey anyone over the age of twenty is old."

Stacey made a face and looked at her watch. "Is it okay if I take my break now?"

The librarian smiled. She was evidently meeting someone. "Of course but don't talk to anyone about what you found until you've spoken to the police."

Hannah knew the girl was bursting to tell anyone who'd listen and she'd probably elaborate the details. A little alarm bell rang.

"Stacey would you mind staying with us? I'd really appreciate your help." Hannah hoped her smile and compliment would win her over without making a fuss about it.

Stacey moved her weight from one foot to the other clearly unable to decide. Nathalie stepped in. "This is your chance to help a journalist, Stacey. A great experience to chalk up."

The girl grinned. "Okay."

Hannah put on a pair of sterile gloves. One thing she didn't want was her fingerprints found on anything. She'd also brought her camera. She studied each photo that Nathalie had placed on a sheet of white paper.

"These look as though they've travelled around a lot." There was a photo of a small boy with two adults, presumably the parents. Another of a man in uniform. One of the woman holding a baby with the small boy standing beside her. All of them were faded. Hannah could almost feel the love and sadness emanating from the images.

Most of the papers were too old and worn to read. Hannah took photographs in the hope that the technical wizards at *The News* could do something with them. There was a folded piece of paper, which seemed recently torn from a notebook which seemed curiously out of context. Opening it they saw just notes which could mean anything:

Children sent to Australia

Nobody wants you at home that's why you're here

Suicides

Drugs

Jail

Abuse

Nothing ever done

Detention centre

Never made a friend

Stole my childhood, identity, heritage

The phone rang on the desk. Nathalie answered it, listened then said, "Thank you. We'll expect you soon then." She replaced the receiver. "That was the police. Someone is coming over to collect these and have a chat with you, Stacey."

"Time to make my exit then. Thank you so much for your help, Stacey. If you remember anything else, Nathalie has my contact details." The girl's face was a picture of disappointment. "But here's my card just in case."

Just for a moment Hannah wondered if she was doing the right thing. She said goodbye to Nathalie. "Thanks and I'll be in touch." The librarian nodded and sat down at her desk in preparation for the police visit.

CHAPTER TWENTY-THREE

Hannah had just enough time to get home and change in time for lunch with Simon. He had phoned to say his case had finished early and he was returning to Manchester that day but would she be able to meet for lunch. This time he invited her to Simpson's on the Strand. Simon certainly enjoyed eating at the best places.

He wasn't there when she arrived but she was shown to a table by the fireplace. It was, the manager informed her, the table Churchill always sat at. Hannah smiled and took her place in history. She had a clear view of the restaurant the seating divided into red for the Lords and green for the Commons.

She picked up the menu and casually studied people at other tables. There was a quiet buzz about the place. A man a few tables away raised his glass to her and she realised she'd been staring at Lord Gyles without realising who it was.

She smiled just as Simon arrived. He turned heads as he made his way across the restaurant.

"Sorry to keep you waiting. I just had a few loose ends to tie up in court." He kissed her cheek and sat down opposite her.

The maître d' placed menus on the table as the wine waiter arrived with a bottle of champagne. "I won my case." He grinned as the waiter poured them each a glass.

Hannah laughed. "Do you ever lose?"

His face clouded momentarily. "The man I wanted to

avoid in Rules. I lost his case with life-changing effects for him. He threatened that he'd ruin me too. I was surprised to see him and wondered –" he broke off to sip his wine.

"Wondered?" Hannah prompted.

"If he was following me. Or rather had had me followed by the man he was with. It was a particularly nasty case. Not the sort of man one would like to be on the wrong side of. I didn't know he was out of prison."

Hannah was relieved that their abrupt departure had had nothing to do with her.

"Anyway I've had a word with a few people… Let's order shall we?"

While they were waiting for their hors d'ouevres, Simon asked, "So how are you getting on with the murdered Aussies?" He laughed at Hannah's expression. "I bumped into Terry Cornhill the other day and he filled me in. You didn't tell me much the other evening."

Hannah wondered how he happened to "bump into" the deputy editor then realised it was none of her business. "There seems to be a connection between them. They were all sent to Australia as part of the Child Migration Scheme. Plus an orphanage called Blackwater House seems to feature in their histories."

"There's a name to conjure with. Bon appetit," Simon said as their starters were placed before them. They ate in silence for a few moments before he said, "You will be careful Hannah, won't you?"

Hannah found it difficult to swallow her smoked salmon. "Why do you say that? Do you know something I don't know?"

"Not directly. But there have been cover-ups over the Child Migration Scheme. Neither the British or Australian government acted totally altruistically."

A waiter took away their plates as another came to their table with the roast beef to be carved. Steaming vegetables arrived and their glasses were replenished with red wine. In such a setting the thought of being in danger seemed preposterous.

"I'm always careful."

"Good to hear. How's your beef?"

The rest of the meal passed in pleasanter conversation until Simon mentioned Lucy Peters. "Strange affair, that. Her brother's death. Did you find out much from those family papers?"

Hannah felt she had been lulled into a false sense of security. Was Simon asking out of friendly curiosity or did he know something she didn't or want to find out what she knew. "Not much at all. Nancy Peters saved so many odd bits of paper, which subsequently her son kept. Of course he may never have actually looked through them. Lucy now seems to think of me as her PA."

Simon laughed loudly causing several people to turn in their direction. He dabbed his mouth with his napkin. "Well she has come up in the world."

Then he absorbed her expression of indignation. "Don't get dragged in." He glanced at his watch and signaled to the maître d'. Their bill arrived and he paid with a credit card. "Sorry Hannah, I have to leave for my train."

They left together and paused on The Strand. Simon

hailed a cab and kissed her cheek. "Hope to see you again soon. Take care."

"You too and thank you for lunch."

"My pleasure." He smiled and for a moment he looked immeasurably sad. Then he was in the taxi and Hannah was left feeling bereft.

Her mobile rang. A call from Lucy. As she was nearby she agreed to pop in to see her before going home.

CHAPTER TWENTY-FOUR

"Someone's following me," Lucy said as soon as she arrived. The comment seemed to have come apropos of nothing and Hannah was taken off-guard.

"What do you mean?" For a moment Hannah had forgotten the photo Edith had taken. The wine at lunch must have dulled her brain.

"Well I'd have thought that was bleedin' obvious. Every time I go out I can feel this presence. I've tried all sorts of tricks but I never see the bastard. He's good."

"He?"

Lucy snorted. "Bound to be a he, isn't it." She lit a cigarette. "Anyway I want you to look into it for me." She blew the smoke away from her guest.

Hannah sighed. She was more than a little fed up with Lucy's increasing and strange demands on her time.

"Lucy I'm a journalist. Not a private detective."

Lucy sniffed eloquently. "Not big enough news then. My brother's dead probably murdered as if you didn't know."

"I do know that. And no one has been found, charged or convicted ..." Hannah was about to say more and thought the better of it. So far her investigations had led her to Wiltshire then... it was strange how many times Australia cropped up in one way or another. "Did any of your family ever emigrate to Australia?" Hannah was thinking of the '£10 Pom' scheme as it was so disparagingly described, designed to populate Australia with white inhabitants. Adults had assisted passage for £10 and their children went free. Thousands had left the UK.

"No idea. Why?"

"Just a thought."

"You don't think my boy went there, do you?" Hannah noticed that Lucy rarely referred to her son by the name he had been given. She wondered what she would have called him.

Hannah chose her words carefully. "Some children in orphanages were sent to Australia as part of what was called the Child Migration Scheme."

Lucy looked at her blankly. "But he wasn't an orphan."

"No he wasn't but I've heard about other children who weren't orphans being sent there."

"Bleedin' hell. Can they do that?"

"It happened. I know of some Australians who have come back to find their families." Hannah didn't mention that they'd died in the attempt.

"You don't think..." Lucy let the thought hang between them. Her face took on a new glow. Then she stared down at her hands and her face sagged. "He wouldn't like what he'd find, would he."

"You don't know that."

"Let's face it, no one would want me as a mother."

"Well that's something we have no control over. But Lucy what happened to you was awful. Your were only a child yourself."

Lucy nodded but looked unconvinced. "I still can't believe Mum lied to me like that. Especially after what happened."

For a moment Hannah wondered how different Lucy's life would have been if they'd kept her child. Lots of children at that time were brought up by grandparents as though their own. But she supposed that had been one step too far for Nancy Peters.

She took Lucy's hand. "We don't know what happened to him. We can only hope that wherever he was, he was placed in a loving family."

Lucy sniffed. "Suppose so." She stared at the photo on the mantelpiece. "I wonder if Harry knew? He was always so secretive about things. And maybe she told him about the baby."

"Did you never talk to Harry about why you went away?"

"Nah." She stared out of the window. "Nothing was ever the same after that. Then I went and stayed with some different nuns. I wasn't a novice but I worked for them. Cleaned and that." She stood up and went to the sideboard, brought out the brandy and the usual gold-rimmed glasses.

"Not for me thanks." Hannah had already had three glasses of wine at lunch and didn't need any more.

"My downfall." Lucy laughed bitterly. "The nuns caught me drinking the communion wine so I was out. It helped kill the pain. I came back to Mum's for a while but... they didn't want me there."

"So what did you do? Where did you go?" Lucy couldn't have spent decades sleeping rough.

She smiled. "Found another convent. Been in and out of them for years."

"But how..." Hannah realised Lucy probably

wouldn't tell her about living on the streets. Yet. "Lucy about being followed..."

Dragged back to the present, Lucy coughed and lit a cigarette. "What about it?"

"You should be careful."

"Well I know that, Einstein. But it's not as though I've got anything worth stealing."

Hannah didn't like to remind her that that was the case for her brother as well but he had been murdered. She wondered what had been stuffed into his mouth after he had died. Someone was keen to leave a message.

CHAPTER TWENTY-FIVE

"Hannah –" it was Rory's voice on the phone – "just had something come in on the wire that I thought you might be interested in."

"A propos of...?"

"Your dead Aussie in the library. There's been another suspicious death."

"Where?"

"Manchester. An Australian male found dead in a pub, it seems."

"Right. Are there any similarities?"

"What apart from them being Aussies? I don't know. We've sent Duncan up there to have a scout around and attend the press briefing. I'll get him to copy you in."

"Thanks Rory. It does seem rather a coincidence. I'll contact the police here to see if they've made the connection if any."

Hannah put the receiver down and sat staring out of the window. Three Australians murdered. Or at least three they knew about. Two in London and now one in Manchester. Why now? And why were they murdered in the UK? To cover up something which happened in Australia? Seemed far-fetched.

She rang Claudia's number only to be told the DI wasn't available. She left her name and number. She wondered about going to Manchester but there seemed little point. The information she'd got about the Dulwich library victim was due to the fact she knew the librarian. She knew no one in Manchester. Idly she leafed through her Filofax. What a shame she didn't add her entries by towns and cities instead of surnames.

She opened a notebook and wrote various headings on a page: school friends; university friends; work contacts. Systematically she went through the lists: school friends she'd kept in contact with. Not many and no one was in Manchester. Likewise her university friends, although that list was longer. No one she'd worked with had flown north either.

Drumming her fingers on the desk, she abruptly stopped when one name popped into her head. Joe Rawlington MP. He was, of course, on her list of university friends but even more importantly he came from Manchester. Or had spent most of his school days there. Was the House of Commons still sitting? She checked the date: 21 July. She dialled up the Internet, ready to send an email to Joe. It was about time she saw him anyway.

Her mobile rang about ten minutes later. "That was quick," Hannah said as she heard Joe's voice.

"How are you? Are you free if I pop over for a drink this evening? We could have a takeaway?"

Hannah had missed Joe of late. She'd loved their long lunches when he'd run his own PR company. They had a shared history that made companionship relaxed. She was thrilled that he and Phil were living together but it did mean she saw less of him. Plus his job as an MP was all-consuming. "That would be lovely."

"See you later then." Joe hung up.

Hannah stretched and for the first time in weeks actually felt relaxed. Joe was such an old friend it would be good to just talk and catch up.

•

Joe arrived bearing wine and a big grin. "I'm celebrating Tony Blair's election to party leader."

"Wow! Come in." They hugged.

"Shall we order a take-away before we catch up?"

Hannah produced the menu and they rang through their order to be delivered. Once they both had a glass of wine in front of them, and they'd toasted the new leader of the opposition, Hannah asked, "What's he like, Tony Blair?"

Joe thought for a moment as though choosing his words carefully. "Intelligent, charismatic, focused, driven."

"Politically sound?"

"I think so." Joe sipped his wine.

"So do you see yourself as part of the new Blair team then?"

Joe shook his head.

"Oh come on you'd be perfect."

"You might very well think that, I couldn't possibly comment." Joe smiled as he echoed the words made famous by the chief whip played by Ian Richardson in the popular *House of Cards* television drama. The sequel, *To Play the King,* just as successful, had been a great favourite with them both the year before.

"Well you ought to be is all I can say."

Joe drank some wine. "Apart from boosting my ego, what else did you want to talk about?"

"Strange you should ask that." Hannah winked. "I want to pick your brains."

Joe laughed. "At least you're honest."

"Did you hear about the Australian man who died in Dulwich library?"

"Can't say I did. It wasn't a major news story, was it?"

"No but it could well be." Hannah poured more wine into their glasses.

"Because…?"

"Because another Australian died in Burgess Park four days before the library one and now one has been found dead, presumably murdered, in Manchester."

"What part of Manchester?"

"Does it make a difference?"

"Could do."

"It was Fallowfield."

"University area. I have an old school friend who lectures there now. If we had the details we could ask her if she knew anyone who could help."

Hannah could feel the bubble of anticipation rising within. She hadn't experienced that for a while and it was the best she'd felt in weeks.

The bell rang and from the monitor, Hannah saw the deliveryman. Joe collected it at the door and they decamped into the dining room together with another bottle of wine.

"How's Phil?"

Joe paused in serving himself some chicken Jalfrezi. "We're both acclimatising ourselves to living together. Sometimes we're too polite with each other, but we're getting there."

"Good. You deserve some happiness."

"And you? How are things with Tom? How was the holiday?'

"Wonderful in some ways. Loved Corfu. Tom had a protection officer with him."

Joe didn't comment.

"He also – " Hannah paused not wishing to be disloyal to Tom but recognising Joe was about the only person she was close enough to, to discuss the problem with. "Tom had terrible nightmares while we were away. Apparently a reaction to what he went through in New York."

"That must have been difficult."

"More than you'd imagine. He's away now – some sort of rehab facility. I don't know where and we're not in contact." Joe was about to say something but she continued, "I do have a number for emergencies."

Joe looked doubtful. "Well that's something I suppose."

Hannah contemplated telling him about her miscarriage but she couldn't face his pity. Not now that she had a buzz of something to work on.

They ate in silence for a few minutes then Joe topped up their glasses. "To new beginnings."

"Yours or mine?" Hannah asked.

"Both."

"Well my new beginning might depend on your contact in Manchester."

"I'll email her when I get home and let you know."

By the time Joe left, Hannah was feeling a lot better. She stacked the plates and glasses in the dishwasher and drank a couple of glasses of water. Hopefully she'd sleep well tonight. She opened the garden door and stood still enjoying the peace. It was only as she was locking up again that she saw a shadow pass by the rear wall in the garden. She froze. Waiting. Nothing or no one emerged so she went upstairs to look in on Elizabeth before getting ready for bed.

The room was lit by a low glow from the nightlight. Elizabeth was peacefully asleep in her cot. As she turned to go she noticed the curtain wasn't closed properly. At the window she thought she saw someone from the house backing on to hers staring across which was impossible in this light. She checked the window locks and pulled the curtain. They were safe. She had to convince herself of that or she'd go mad.

CHAPTER TWENTY-SIX

The next morning Hannah was at her desk, thinking about Lucy. If her brother had been killed, could she also be at risk, as she feared? She thought it unlikely that she was being followed but there was that photograph taken by Edith... The telephone rang.

"Hi Hannah, sorry it's taken me so long to get back to you. I've been out of town." DI Claudia Turner's telephone conversations were always terse as though she expected someone to be listening in.

"Manchester by any chance?"

"Yes, as it happens."

"I was thinking of making a visit myself."

"I'd save yourself the train fare."

"Well, I'm waiting for a contact to get back to me. Do you think there's a connection between the three deaths?"

"Not really, except that all the men came from Australia." There was a pause as Claudia could be heard talking to someone in her office. "Do you have time for a drink this evening? We could compare notes. I could pop over after seven if that suits?"

Hannah agreed and hung up. It would be interesting to hear what the DI had discovered in Manchester and it might save her a journey. Then she dismissed that thought. She needed face-to-face conversations and impressions, which might produce new leads. However she was grateful that Claudia seemed happy to share information.

While she was thinking about this Rory rang. "Just getting some details of the Manchester death faxed over to you. Duncan said the police were downplaying it. Could be natural causes etc. But the curious thing – of maybe not – is that this man was also researching his family history."

"Isn't that what Aussies do? Look for their forebears in the old country?"

"That's rather dismissive, Ms Weybridge, if I may say so."

"Not really just playing Devil's advocate. Maybe it's linked to children – orphans – being sent off to Australia."

"Makes sense in that they were looking for family. But why would they be killed? Anyway the faxes should be with you imminently."

Hannah unplugged the phone-line she used for the Internet and plugged in the fax machine. A few minutes later it rang and printouts arrived.

Claudia Turner arrived a little after seven bearing her usual offering of wine. As always she was smartly dressed – her pale blue linen suit only slightly creased after a day's wear. "You look better than the last time I saw you." She smiled as Hannah came back into the room with glasses and corkscrew. She was wearing a pretty cotton frock, and was her usual groomed self.

"I am, thanks."

Claudia didn't miss the shadow of sadness that passed over Hannah's face but refrained from comment.

"So how was your trip to Manchester? Do you think the deaths are linked?"

"There are some similarities and differences. All the men are Australians but have been living in different regions. Although we're having difficulty tracing any family for our one in the library, it seems the Manchester man had come over with his wife and has two children back in Oz. Both at university. Maybe you'd get something out of the wife, Hannah."

"Oh?" Hannah had already made an appointment to see the widow the next day. The faxes she'd received had included details of the wife. As luck would have it she had arrived in London to stay with some relatives she had there.

"Don't look like that." Claudia laughed and poured some more wine. "You know how people are drawn to you. You're not seen as threatening. People are often hostile to or reserved with the police."

"I can't imagine why." Hannah remembered being questioned by DS Benton when she'd discovered Liz's body in the church crypt. Benton had made it seem as though she were personally responsible for her friend's death.

Claudia ignored that remark. "And you're a journalist known for getting to the bottom of things."

Hannah wasn't convinced. "I don't like the way some stories become so personal."

"Meaning?"

"Like you don't know." Hannah searched for the right words. "Claudia, you're always distanced in your role. Somehow my life ends up entangled in the stories I'm investigating."

Claudia nodded. She commiserated but since Hannah

had been instrumental in clearing up some complex cases, she valued the journalist's input. She managed to see things from a different perspective to the police enquiries. She took nothing at face value but she often found herself in serious trouble.

"How do you do it? It can't be easy as a female DI."

Claudia studied her wine glass for a moment as though her life were reflected there. "Always have to be one jump ahead. Never let down my guard."

"That must be exhausting. When I worked on women's magazines, the staff was mainly female but I wouldn't say there was much solidarity. Georgina must face similar problems to you editing *The News*." Claudia didn't reply. "I interviewed a female fire-fighter a couple of years ago. The overt sexism she faced both within the service and from the public was horrendous."

Claudia nodded but said nothing.

"Apparently at one house fire she attended a man refused to be carried out by her."

"And?"

"She told him he either went with her or could burn with the house."

Claudia laughed. "Good for her."

They were both silent for a moment. Then Hannah asked, "Is anything happening about Harry Peters' death?"

Claudia looked surprised. "Why?"

Hannah sighed. "I know this sounds unkind but his sister Lucy seems to regard me as her personal factotum.

Last thing was to help with organising his funeral. I'm not responsible for her but she has a way of making me feel as though I am."

"Difficult." Claudia topped up their glasses. "Is there anything I should know?"

Hannah contemplated revealing the missing child Lucy had given birth to. But it seemed such a breech of trust. "She thinks she's being followed."

"And is she, in your opinion?"

"Who knows? She said that as her brother was killed she might be next. And we know from Edith's photos that someone was keeping a watch on Harry. And Lucy. Did you find anything out about that ring?"

"No. Did you?"

Hannah shook her head. "I don't know where to start to be honest."

"We need an expert in religious imagery or icons or something to …" she didn't finish her sentence.

"Yes, I should try a couple of my contacts." She paused as if thinking about who she should approach then asked, "Have you seen Tom?"

Claudia nearly spilt the wine. "Where did that come from? No I haven't. Have you?"

"I thought I did." Hannah's face betrayed the hurt she had felt as she stared at the other woman.

"Where? How?" Claudia looked genuinely shocked and puzzled.

"In the Horseferry Pub after I'd been to the funeral directors with Lucy. I saw him in the other bar but he disappeared before I could reach him."

"You sure it really was him? Not wishful thinking?"

"Wishful thinking would have had him acknowledge me."

"I suppose it would. But truthfully Hannah I've not seen or heard from him – and I've not heard anything about him on the grapevine either."

"Thank you. You will tell me if you do, won't you?"

"I promise." Claudia drained her glass. "And please let me know if you get any leads on these Australian deaths."

Hannah nodded but did not mention she was seeing the widow of the Manchester victim on the following day.

CHAPTER TWENTY-SEVEN

The wooden gate creaked in protest as Hannah opened it and took the few steps to the front door, which was painted a canary yellow and glistened in the sunshine. She pressed the bell and heard a murmur of voices from within before the door was opened by a man wearing shorts and a t-shirt bearing the slogan: *The Taste that Unites Us* above a picture of a cup of tea. Hannah wondered at the choice of attire.

"Hi I'm Hannah Weybridge. I arranged to meet Mrs Smarley here."

The man, who appeared to be in his forties, stared at her for a moment. No welcoming smile. "You'd better come in then." He led the way down the hall and opened a door into what was a combined 'family' room and kitchen, which was lit with bright sunshine coming in via the patio windows.

A woman sitting in a wicker chair stood up and held out her hand. "I'm Melanie Smarley. You must be the journalist." Her voice betrayed only a slight Australian accent.

"I am. Hannah Weybridge and I'm very sorry for your loss, Mrs Smarley."

"Please call me Mel." The two women shook hands and Hannah took the seat indicated.

"Would you like some coffee or a cold drink?"

"Water would be great thank you."

They settled into their seats and Hannah observed the other woman's face. Her grief shrouded her. Her skin was blotchy and her eyes looked as though they were about to disappear into their sockets. She clutched a screwed up, damp tissue in her hand.

"You're not how I imagined you."

Hannah was thrown by the statement, which seemed to come out of nowhere. But it was as good an icebreaker as any other. She smiled. "How did you imagine me?"

"Oh I don't know. Fierce I think."

"Fierce? Why?" Hannah could never imagine herself as fierce.

Melanie was quiet for a moment. "I hear you've been involved in investigations that have threatened your own life. You don't look as though you'd hold your own fighting your way out of a paper bag."

Hannah nearly laughed. "Appearances can be deceptive. But I am here to fight your corner, Mel, if you'll let me?" Melanie nodded. "Could you tell me about the background to your husband's visit to the UK?"

A tear slid down the widow's face. The screwed-up tissue wiped it away. "We were never enough." The words, quietly spoken, conveyed the depth of her heartbreak.

"I'm sorry?"

"We were never enough for him. Our family. Our children. Len wanted to know his roots and to discover why he'd been shipped out to Australia. He felt betrayed by his UK family." She paused long enough to sip her drink. "When we met he was recovering from a severe depression. He was a very damaged person. On arrival in Australia he'd been sent to some religious institution where the children had been made to do physical work under horrendous conditions. Work which would have been exacting for grown men." She stared out of the window. An English garden in summer was a far cry from what Len had experienced as an immigrant.

Hannah waited for her to continue.

"The boys were abused sexually, physically and mentally. It took Len years before he could tell me about it. When we met he ... he was haunted. And angry. Angry that his family hadn't wanted him. That's what the children were told: your families don't want you. No one wants you."

Hannah was struck by the echo from Jeff Collins' notes. "Do you remember the name of the religious institution?"

Mel closed her eyes for a few seconds. "No not properly. It was some sort of Brotherhood, I think. Something to do with Pilgrims."

Hannah hardly dared to breathe. "Could it have been the Christian Brotherhood of the Holy Pilgrims?"

Mel stared at her. "It could. But I'm not one hundred per cent sure. I think Len kept some documents at home. I'll check if he brought any notes with him. His anger at his treatment never abated."

Hannah wanted her to check there and then but Mel didn't move. There was a softening of her expression.

"But there was another side to him," she continued, "that was loving and caring in spite of what he'd been through. He was a wonderful father and husband. But there was always this space, this emptiness, an extra part of him that... Anyway the children are at university and when Bill received a redundancy payment we agreed to come to the UK to see what we could discover about his birth family."

Hannah was making notes on her pad. "And he knew to go to Manchester because?"

"He'd kept a scrap of paper when he was shipped over. They all wore labels. Appalling like parcels or bags of laundry. Anyway on one side it was inscribed Manchester, Piccadilly Station." She paused to blow her nose noisily. "We'd been there two weeks when he made a breakthrough and found some members of the Smarley family who thought they could be connected. Jim arranged to meet them – he didn't want me to go with him – and that's when it happened. He was sitting outside the pub waiting."

Hannah wondered if she would ever become immune to seeing other people's raw grief. It put her own into perspective. But the empathy she felt moved her to clasp Melanie's hand.

"What actually happened?"

"Well it seems he had a heart attack. So cruel when he was so close to finding out…" Her sobs completed the sentence.

"Have you had any contact with the family, Mel?"

"Yes I met his older brother – he was the one my husband was going to meet. He was shocked. He said he was glad they hadn't told his mother. She's very frail, apparently."

Hannah pondered this information. "If you don't mind my asking, Mel do you know anything about their financial situation?"

"No why?" A light dawned in her eyes. "Please don't think we were doing this for any sort of financial gain." Her fury was evident. "We're doing alright with the redundancy payment and we have shares in a family business. We're not seeking out these British relatives cap in hand."

Hannah studied her flushed face. "I didn't for a moment think you were." She paused. "What I do wonder is ... if the family thought you might be and they wanted to protect their inheritance." She let that thought find its level.

Mel looked aghast. "You can't think ..." she didn't finish her sentence.

"Well it's one line of thought. What have the police said?"

"Nothing much. They seem to want to write it off as natural causes but Len never had any problems with his health."

"I assume you are getting some support from the Australian Embassy?"

Mel wiped her eyes with the dirty tissue. Hannah wanted to tell her to use a clean one but managed to refrain. "Yes they've been very supportive. My cousins here have been so kind." Her eyes welled up again. "I don't know what to do for the best. My children want to come over but they have their studies and until we sort out..."

What needed sorting out was cut short by two teenagers barging through the door, trying to trip each other up in their eagerness to get to the fridge. Their mother followed. "I am so sorry Mel – they just didn't think." She glared at the boys who attempted to look remorseful.

Hannah took this as her cue to leave. She handed Mel her card. "You can contact me at any time. Even if I can't help, I may be able to find someone who can."

"Thank you." Melanie put the card in the bag by her side and took out an envelope. "Here's a recent photo of Len. Just in case you need one."

"Thank you. And I'll let you know if I uncover anything." The widow nodded.

"I'll see you out." The cousin closed the door behind them. "Do you think Len's death is suspicious?"

"I don't know but there have been two other Australian men killed recently. There could be a link. However it might just be a cruel coincidence." Hannah smiled. "I won't intrude…"

"Right." The woman paused. "Did Mel tell you that Len had thought he was being followed?"

Hannah shook her head.

"It was the day before he died, apparently. He had the impression that someone had been following him all day. I only met Len once but he seemed a straightforward type not given to flights of fancy. I'm sure if he thought he was being followed, then he was. I'm surprised she didn't mention it."

"Grief does strange things to our memories. Some people recall the tiniest details, others forget even the major ones." She smiled at the woman. "I'm sorry I didn't catch your name?"

"Joanne – Jo."

Hannah gave her a business card. "Perhaps you'd call

me if you think of anything else."

Jo turned the card over, looking thoughtful. "I will," she said as she opened the front door and Hannah left wondering about who had been following Len Smarley and why.

As she made her way home, Hannah wondered for the umpteenth time why these deaths were happening now? Although they had been made to look like natural deaths, there were too many to be coincidental. But why now? As far as she could see, and she'd been in contact with a social worker in Nottingham who had been investigating children sent to Australia, and supporting a steady stream of these adults coming back to the UK, looking for their families. None of those had died. However some had discovered that their parents or siblings were sadly no longer alive.

What did these particular men – and they were all men (so far she added to herself) – have in common? The three she knew about had all come from different parts of Queensland. One hadn't married, one was divorced and one had come over with his wife. The common factor was an age range of fifty to sixty years. So that meant they had left the UK on some of the early migration project ships.

Back in her study she drafted her first article that was little more than a long news item, naming the three men and tentatively linking them to the Child Migration Scheme. She didn't feel able to include the name of the religious institution Jeff Collins had been to. And that Len may have been sent to. There were more questions than answers but she hoped that the article might stir some memories. Hannah had asked Sheila about the possibility of including her cousin's name as someone who had been sent off to the other side of the world but she wanted to hold fire on that. It was a difficult call, Hannah knew, and Janet, with whom Hannah had discussed the idea, had thought her relative wouldn't have welcomed the publicity.

She checked through all her notes. This religious establishment had a lot to answer for. Was the Brotherhood still a power to be reckoned with? And if so would their involvement lead to murder?

CHAPTER TWENTY-EIGHT

"Hey Hannah," one of the subs called across the newsroom, "there's a guy in reception who would like to have a word with you."

Hannah looked across at Rory. "Want me to come down with you?" he asked.

The weight of the past had to be shrugged off some time. "No it's fine, thanks." She picked up her bag and made for the lifts. When the doors opened on the ground floor, she emerged to see a man striding towards her. His suit was well cut, the grey in his hair gave him a distinguished appearance and when he smiled the lines round his eyes deepened.

"Ms Weybridge?" His voice reminded her of someone whom she couldn't quite place but he didn't look familiar. How did he know her?

He held out his hand. "Colin Helmswood." He paused as though he expected her to know his name.

Hannah took his outstretched hand. It was warm and the skin felt soft. She noticed his hands were well cared for. Manicured nails. "How do you do?"

Colin Helmswood smiled. "Sorry to barge into your day but I wanted to have a word with you." He made it sound like he was speaking to one of his subordinates. Hannah bristled.

"And you couldn't do that on the phone?" She realised too late how rude that sounded. "I'm sorry Mr Helmswood, I didn't intend that to sound so offensive."

"Please call me Colin and no offence taken." He

seemed to be staring into her. Absorbing her. Hannah felt uncomfortable and at the same time intrigued.

"Well, Colin, how can I help you?"

He considered for a moment. "Is there somewhere we could talk privately?"

Reception was getting busier as people left the building for lunch. There was an interview room on this floor just behind reception. Hannah approached the security man at the desk to ask if the room was free. It was.

"Would you just like to sign in? We can use the interview room."

Colin Helmswood signed the visitors' book and followed Hannah through the security gate into a nondescript room furnished with four armchairs around a coffee table. The arrangement of flowers was the only alleviation from dull. There was a coffee machine on a counter. And a variety of mugs. Hannah had never used the room before and wondered what the protocol was.

Helmswood sat in one of the chairs and leaned forward as Hannah sat opposite him. "So why did you want to meet me?"

Colin considered his nails for a long moment. "I think, Hannah, I may be a target for this murderer."

Hannah stared. "Which murderer?"

"The one who is killing off these men from Australia? I read your piece yesterday. I know what the connection is between them. And I could be next."

Hannah was deep in thought as she walked back to her desk some time later. What Colin Helmswood had revealed made some sort of warped sense but there was something niggling at the back of her mind. Something that made her suspicious. Plus the fact that he recognised her. From where? She was sure they hadn't met before.

"So why are you telling me all this, Colin? Why not go to the police?"

Colin studied her face. "I've been following your career."

"I'm sorry?" Acid rose in her throat. His tone of voice sounded like a threat. There were too many people who thought they could manipulate her. Following. Why?

"I've obviously expressed myself badly." The well-modulated tones jarred with Hannah but she kept her expression to what she hoped was neutral. "What I meant was that I've followed your previous exposés which were explosive and when I read your recent article about the unexplained deaths of Australian men researching their family histories..." he left the sentence unfinished as though it explained itself.

Hannah sat at her desk and sent an email to the cuttings department requesting anything on Colin Helmswood. He was definitely holding back and she was curious as to what and why. She turned over the business card he had given her. All it revealed was his name, email address and a mobile phone number. It was the type of card you could get printed off cheaply in one of those quick print places. And revealed nothing about him. But one fact he did reveal – he too had been sent to The Christian Brotherhood of the Holy Pilgrims.

The cuttings department came back with nothing on

Colin Helmswood. Hannah decided on a short cut and phoned Claudia to see if they had anything on him.

"Sorry, Hannah, the DI isn't available at the moment. Will I do?"

Mike Benton sounded friendliness personified and she wondered why.

"It's another favour, Mike. I've just had someone come to see me at *The News*, claiming he could be a target for the person killing the Australian men. He said he was sent out to Australia on the Child Migration Scheme but returned to the UK as a young adult. What he says does tally with what I've uncovered about the other victims."

"But?" Benton wondered not for the first time how Hannah always managed to get a different slant on things.

"But something's not quite right. I think he's stringing me a line."

"So you would like me to run his name through our system?"

"If you would. His name is Colin Helmswood. I took a photograph which is just being developed then I could fax it over to you."

"That would help. How did you get the pic?"

Hannah laughed. "Without him knowing."

Hannah left the office in a lighter frame of mind and was almost looking forward to the evening ahead.

CHAPTER TWENTY-NINE

The evening was perfect for an outdoor reception and the Kensington Roof Gardens was the ideal venue. The fountain in the centre was under-lit with coloured lights giving it a magical air complemented by the string quartet in one corner playing Handel's Water Music. Waiters moved unobtrusively among the guests bearing trays of Champagne or canapés and conversations cascaded.

Hannah had not been surprised to receive an invitation from Lord Gyles who was celebrating another newspaper launch. But she was thrown that it included a plus one. And at such short notice. She had thought about declining, which was out of the question, then about going on her own but that felt too exposing. In the end she asked James if he would accompany her. She hadn't seen him for a while – he worked such long hours as a junior hospital doctor – and their conversation was stilted.

"I'm sorry Hannah, I'd love to but I'm on nights all that week. But we must get together soon."

"Yes, it's been too long." She felt friendless and alone.

"Why don't you ask my neighbour Mark? He's back flat-sitting again and I'll bet he'd jump at the chance of a posh do."

"D'you think so?" Hannah was rapidly running out of options. Joe and Phil were otherwise engaged and Tom was obviously never on the cards.

"I should think so. I'll get him to call you. Sorry, got

to go." And that was that. But two hours later Mark rang.

"Hi Hannah, James explained he needed a stand-in and I'd be happy to escort you." That sounded distinctly old fashioned but he was more than presentable and so she agreed.

"That very kind of you, Mark. It's a black tie do but should be fun."

When Mark had called to collect her earlier that evening she almost didn't recognise him. He looked ... handsome, debonair, sophisticated.

"You look gorgeous," he'd said observing her green silk dress, which had been an absolute treat for herself to herself. A consolation prize she thought.

Now Mark passed her a glass of champagne and smiled. 'The last time I was here was for a wedding reception –" he laughed at Hannah's expression – "no need to look so surprised. We military like to push the boat out as well, you know."

He glanced around and Hannah felt he was sizing up the room, the guests, the situation. Always on duty she thought.

She was about to reply when the maître d' announced the toasts and everyone fell silent. Lord Gyles stepped forward to welcome his guests and make a self-deprecatory speech about his achievements, which had led to enlarging his media empire plus his election to the Press Complaints Commission.

There was enthusiastic applause and guests raised their glasses. Hannah realised she hadn't listened to a word that was spoken. Rory was beside her. "Hannah?" She stared at him for a moment then she was in the present again.

"Hi Rory let me introduce to Mark who gallantly agreed to accompany me this evening."

"I wouldn't have thought that was too much of a hardship." The two men shook hands and Hannah thought she saw a glimmer of recognition between them. But then put it down to the imaginings of wine.

The bell rang for dinner and they checked for a seating plan. There wasn't one. Guests were making their way to the buffet and then sitting ad hoc at tables. It was informal – at odds with their attire. Mark and Hannah waited for the queue to subside before going to the buffet. They sat at a table and were immediately joined by a couple who bore all the signs of having had a huge row. They ate methodically, in silence.

"Good evening Hannah. How lovely to see you on such a joyful occasion."

The News' legal expert Larry Jefferson pulled over a chair and sat near them. The other couple looked up but said nothing. Hannah made the introductions and Larry smiled at Mark. "Ah, yes, the citizen's arrest chap. I remember Hannah telling me about your swift reaction in Lordship Lane. Good to meet you. I trust this evening is a pleasant change from your work in … Bosnia, isn't it?"

Mark laughed. "Indeed. Although your metaphorical mine fields must be as dangerous as mine."

The older man assessed the military man. "Never that, dear man. I'm not half so brave. Hannah, here, is another story."

The silent couple hung on every word.

"You flatter me." She remembered the time when this man had been so hateful to her when the newspaper bought her story about the prostitutes' scandal and then spiked it. Since then he'd become more of an ally. And she'd grown to respect him.

Larry drained his glass. "Oh well better earn my keep and circulate." He smiled at Hannah and Mark. "Enjoy your evening."

The woman of the silent couple considered them strangely. "Are you Hannah Weybridge?"

Hannah considered denying her identity. "Yes I..." before she could say any more there was a scrape of chairs and Mark had deflected a full glass of red wine which the woman had aimed at Hannah. He clenched the woman's wrist as a waiter rushed over to clear the broken glass and spilt wine.

"You're hurting me, let go." Mark released her. She turned to Hannah. "That was for a friend." And with that she turned to her husband. "Come on we're leaving."

Hannah was shaking. The waiter refilled their glasses and melted into the background.

"What on earth was that about?" Rory had joined them.

"Do you know who they are?" Hannah asked.

"Haven't a clue. But remind me to sit near you if I happen to offend anyone Mark."

Hannah stared at Rory. "But who's her friend? Who have I offended?"

"I wouldn't let it get to you. She was drunk and

was determined to cause a scene. Good thing Mark was here." He smiled but Hannah knew he wouldn't leave it there. He would have an answer for her. And his expression made Hannah feel he had some sort of inkling already.

Lord Gyles had arranged a fleet of taxis to take his guests home. Hannah was grateful for Mark's silence in the car. She was tired. She was so used to spending time alone or with Elizabeth that being sociable was exhausting, she found. Or she was just out of practice.

"Thanks for inviting me."

"A pleasure. Thanks for saving my dress from a red wine desecration."

Mark chuckled. "Glad to be of service." He picked up her hand. "I hope you might join me for a meal soon in a less ostentatious venue?"

"That would be nice." She hoped her voice didn't betray her thoughts. Having a dinner à deux couldn't be further from her mind. Romantic complications she could do without.

Mark got out of the car when it pulled up outside her door but she needn't have worried. He saw her to her door, kissed her on the cheek and stood at the gate until she was safely inside.

Janet looked up from the book she was reading. "Nice evening?"

Hannah flopped on to the other settee. "Interesting. Think I'm losing the knack of socialising. I'm exhausted."

"Need to get back into the swing of it then." Janet

stood up. "All's well with Elizabeth."

"Thanks. See you tomorrow. Would you like a cab home?"

"No it's a nice evening and I could do with stretching my legs."

Hannah locked the door after her, switched on the alarm and went into the kitchen for a glass of water. It was true she was out of the habit of socialising. Maybe she should organise a dinner party – if she could think of enough people to invite. She laughed at herself and went upstairs.

Elizabeth was sleeping soundly in her cot. One arm was stretched above her head and the other clutched her favourite teddy. Whenever she looked at her daughter like this she felt almost overwhelmed by love and tenderness. Elizabeth moved slightly and mumbled as Hannah stroked her cheek almost willing her to wake. Then chided herself for her selfishness.

In her bedroom as she slipped off her dress she noticed the tiniest splash of red wine. It looked like blood and she froze remembering the scene at the table. If it hadn't been for Mark the situation would have been a lot worse. Who was that woman and more to the point who was the friend on whose behalf she was acting? Judy Barton crossed her mind. Not a pleasant thought to go to sleep on.

CHAPTER THIRTY

"Have you noticed the woman at number 35?"

Hannah shook her head, her mouth full of Leah's lemon drizzle cake. She swallowed. "No why?"

"She's pregnant again." Hannah had gradually got to know her neighbour who lived on the opposite side of her road. Leah had confided in her that she had always wanted children but had never managed to conceive. It was, she said, a disappointment and sadness that hadn't lessened over the years. Hannah didn't think of Leah as a bitter or jealous woman and wondered at her tone. She felt uncomfortable given her recent experience. "How many children does she have now?"

"Too many. She always seems to be pregnant." She stared into her coffee cup. "That's an exaggeration I know and not what I wanted to talk about."

"Oh?" Hannah was surprised that there was an ulterior motive for Leah's invitation. She enjoyed the times they had coffee together and her cakes were to die for. Leah was the nearest thing she had to a friend in her road.

Her hostess looked flustered. "Could I ask you to check something for me?" She misjudged her guest's expression and added, "I mean can I hire you to investigate something or rather someone for me?"

Hannah smiled. "I'd be happy to check something or someone for you, Leah. You don't have to pay me." She paused. "Unless..."

"Yes?"

"Unless you'd like to make me one of your fabulous lemon drizzle cakes."

"I'd do that anyway. More coffee?" Hannah nodded.

"The thing is I've received a rather strange letter from a man in Australia. He claims to be a relative although I've never heard of him. That isn't to say he isn't, of course. Hannah are you okay?"

Hannah was staring at her. "I'm sorry." She put the piece of cake, which was halfway to her mouth, back on the plate. "It's just what you just said is such a coincidence."

Leah looked bemused. "Really? Why?"

"May I see the letter?"

Leah got up and retrieved a letter from the kitchen counter. "I left it here just in case." She smiled as she handed over an airmail envelope.

Hannah wiped her fingers on the napkin by her plate and slipped out the flimsy paper. She read the letter through quickly and could feel the tingle of the story shaping in her mind. It was more interesting for what it didn't say than what it did which was a brief outline of how Adam Baylis came to be in Australia via the Child Migration Scheme. He had been adopted by a farmer and his wife who were now dead. When going through their papers he discovered his original documents and began researching his family with the help of his son who was now living in London. He shared a surname with Leah before she married and was tentatively asking if she had any relatives who might remember him.

"Well, what do you think?" Leah poured more coffee and Hannah noticed that her hands were trembling. She considered what she was going to say. She didn't want to alarm Leah with a mention of the deaths of Australian men, as she obviously hadn't read her article in *The News*. On the other hand...

"The coincidence I was talking about – I have been looking into the Child Migration Scheme as part of another story I'm working on. But also someone else asked me to investigate the disappearance of a cousin just after the war."

"So could you help me with this?"

"I'll do my best. Would you be happy for me to include this in my articles – if it comes to anything?"

Leah hesitated. "I think so. I suppose if the man is genuine he would be happy to have his story publicised. It might find more family connections for him."

"Would you like me to contact his son? Maybe that would help shed more light before you get involved."

Leah let out a long breath. "That would be so kind. I trust your judgement completely. As you can see, Adam Baylis hasn't given the son's Scott's address but he does say where he works. It's a bar in Soho."

"I'm not being totally altruistic, you know. This young man might be able to help me as well." Hannah didn't want Leah to think she was some sort of angel – avenging or otherwise.

"Two for the price of one, then." Leah smiled. "I'll bake your cake."

The George Pub was dark after the bright sunshine outside. It wasn't busy and there was only one person behind the bar – a woman with the air of someone who ran the place. She was dressed smartly in a fitted, brick pink dress, which matched her lipstick. Her hennaed hair was permed. Hannah smiled, perched on one of the bar stools and asked for a glass of white wine. "And whatever you're drinking."

The woman smiled. "Thanks." She poured two glasses of white wine. "So how can I help you?"

"I'm looking for Scott, I think he works here."

"And you're looking for him because?" The woman was curiously hostile but then why should she divulge anything about her staff to a stranger?

"I'm a friend of a friend of his father, Adam, Adam Baylis."

The woman wiped the bar with a cloth although it seemed not to need it in Hannah's eyes. "You're not the Old Bill then?"

Hannah laughed. "Far from it. Just helping out a neighbour." She raised her glass to the woman then sipped her wine. The woman moved along the bar to serve another customer. Hannah didn't turn but watched the exchange in the huge mirror behind the optics. The man's face was turned away from her. The woman took his money and returned his change before coming back to Hannah and her own drink.

"So friend of a friend, here's your man." The woman nodded in the direction of a tall, slim man in his early twenties who had walked into the bar.

"G'day Rose, sorry I'm late." His Australian drawl and his deliberate, lazy stroll antagonised his boss.

The woman looked at her watch. "Don't make a habit of it."

The young man took up his position behind the bar. "Well, you're not exactly run off your feet, mate."

Hannah winced.

"Then you can make up the time when we are."

"No worries."

"This lady would like a word with you." Rose tactfully moved away to the other end of the bar.

He gave her a questioning look. "I'm sorry, do I know you?"

"No you don't but I think your father is Adam Baylis?"

"Yes. Is he okay? Nothing's happened has it?" He appeared terrified and Hannah wondered if the man was ill.

"As far as I know your father is fine." Hannah smiled. "He sent a letter to a friend of mine mentioning that you were helping him to try and trace his family."

His face broke into a wide grin. "You don't say. He wrote to her then. Good on him. Does she remember him? The parents are dead. I established that but I think they had a daughter as well." Hannah admired the way he drip-fed his information.

"She doesn't remember him." His face fell. "But that doesn't mean to say other people in her family won't be able to help. She would just like some more details."

"Sure. It's my day off tomorrow. Could we meet up and I'll bring everything I have to show you?"

Hannah made a quick calculation. "I work for a newspaper Scott, would you be able to come to the offices? We could make copies of anything if necessary and might be able to help with some of the research."

Hannah gave him her business card. "Could you meet

me there at eleven tomorrow morning?"

He turned the card over in his hand. Hannah thought she saw a glimmer of recognition but then chided herself. Her name was hardly famous and certainly not to an Aussie working as a barman. "Thanks." He scribbled on a beer mat. "Here's my number just in case anything changes."

"Where are you staying?"

He laughed. "A share house in Earls Court. Where else?" He wrote some more on the mat. "There you go."

Hannah finished her drink. "See you tomorrow then. Thank you," she called over to Rose who acknowledged her with a wave.

As she left she noticed that the only other client in the pub, nursing a half pint of beer, seemed very interested in her departure. In the gloom she couldn't make out much about the person but the feeling was there. Of being watched and it was not a comfortable sensation.

Outside she crossed the road and ducked into an alleyway. Seconds later the person who had been observing her emerged. He stared up and down the street, then marched off in the direction she would have taken, suggesting that he knew where she had come from. Hannah was relieved to see a black cab with its light on and plunged into its safety.

CHAPTER THIRTY-ONE

Although Hannah had expected him to be late, Scott Baylis arrived promptly at *The News'* East London offices. She had arranged to use the meeting room on her floor. Rory was at hand in case she needed some more input and the secretary had been briefed that she might be required to make some photocopies. Hannah met him at the lifts. He looked relaxed in a way only Aussie men seemed to have, smiling at everyone as they made their way through the open plan section and arriving at the glass office.

"Tea? Coffee?" Hannah was itching to see what he had brought but reminded herself to observe the social niceties.

"Coffee would be great." He folded himself into a seat and placed his bag on the table. "What's she like?" Hannah was thrown for a moment as she poured the coffees. "Leah Braithwaite. Now that's a name to conjure with." He grinned at her.

"She's a very special lady who I'm very fond of."

"Which is why you're acting on her behalf."

"Yes although your story does tie in with something else I'm working on."

"Really?" He seemed a bit put out.

Hannah passed him the coffee. "Tell me about your father."

"There are two versions. The one he told us, I mean the family, and what I have since discovered. I majored in law and came over here to see if we could find out about Dad's family. The bar job is just to keep me going. And I've made some good contacts." He sipped his coffee and made a face. "Got any sugar?" Hannah got up and collected some sachets and handed them to him. Scott took his time stirring three sachets into his coffee.

"Mum and Dad have a property in Queensland. A farm. It's Mum's really. Her family took dad in when he was sent over as part of the Child Migration Project after the war. We'd always assumed he was an orphan and my grandparents brought him up as their own. They'd always wanted a son. What they didn't expect was that their daughter and adopted son would fall in love. At first they tried to dissuade them but in the end love triumphed and all that." He paused to drink his coffee.

Hannah had been recording their conversation and making notes at the same time. "Sounds like a success story for the Child Migration Scheme."

"You'd think so wouldn't you? Over the last few years at home there have been stories in the press that some of those children were not, in fact, orphans. And some of them ended up in some terrible places run by extreme religious groups. They were abused mentally and physically. People have tried to cover up the worst cases but shit has a way of rising. Anyway the long and the short of it is dad started wondering if he had any family here. And if so why was he sent away? He vaguely remembered his parents."

Hannah nodded. She was thinking about the man who died in the library. The man she now knew as Jeff Jones.

"So –" Scott opened his bag. "Here's a copy of Dad's original birth certificate. I traced his parents and they are both dead. However they weren't dead when Dad left the country. His dad was in hospital and my dad's mum, my grandmother, had a new baby and couldn't manage everything on her own so dad was taken into care on a temporary basis. Two weeks later he was shipped to Australia."

"Do you know what happened? Did the parents try to trace him?"

"No idea. I did find that the baby they had was a girl. Called Leah. I found out she'd married and was living in London. I told dad about everything I'd found and gave him the address I'd got for his sister. I'm so pleased he wrote to her."

"You've done some good detecting work." Hannah noticed Scott's expression. "I'm not being patronising, I'm complimenting you. Your father was circumspect in his letter. He didn't say he thought he and Leah were siblings."

"Good for him. I've done some more digging since I told my dad. I found my dad's aunt who's still alive – the last survivor of that generation it seems. She told me that when her brother came out of hospital he went with his wife to get his child back only to be told he had died. Apparently they never really recovered. They didn't have any more children. They adored Leah, of course, but they never forgave themselves about Adam. The aunt, my great aunt, thought they died early because of their grief. They had moved away from where they were known and never told Leah she'd had a brother."

Hannah paused the tape. "Wow that's a lot to take in. Could I photocopy all these documents?"

Scott nodded. "Any chance of another coffee?"

At that moment Rory poked his head around the door. "Nearly lunchtime Hannah." It was her cue to get rid of her interviewee if she needed to.

"Okay. How about a beer instead of a coffee, Scott? And something to eat."

"Now you're talking. Am I pleased you interrupted," he said standing up to shake Rory's hand. "I thought she was going to keep me talking here for ever. My throat feels like ..."

After Hannah had given the pile of documents to the secretary to be photocopied, they decamped to the Pen & Ink. Rory got their drinks and brought over the menu, which Scott scanned and chose fish and chips. "That okay for you as well, Hannah?" She nodded and Rory went to order.

"Has your father told you anything about his arrival in Australia. When he was a child?"

"Nah only that he thought he'd got lucky. There was a sort of group, which got some of them together years later. Most of them had been sent to some religious institutions." Scott took a gulp of beer. "My dad didn't go into details but what I gather is that they were systematically abused. They were forced to do manual work, which nearly killed them. Some of them never recovered. Apparently some ended up in prison. Most got into drugs. Many ended their own lives." He paused. "You can see why my dad thought he'd been one of the fortunate ones."

Rory returned. "Food won't be long."

Hannah had been making some notes and smiled. "Scott, do you think your father would speak to me?"

Scott laughed. "After you've helped him connect with Leah? Damn sure he would. I'll email him from your office if that's okay?"

Walking back to the office, Rory and Scott were engrossed in a conversation about the latest Test Match between South Africa and England. England had lost much to Rory's chagrin. Hannah let their voices flow in and out of her consciousness until she realised they had both stopped talking and walking so that she almost bumped into them.

"Hannah?" Rory looked concerned. "Think we need to get a move on."

Back in the office, Scott sat at her desk to use the computer to email his father. It was unlikely he would hear back from him for some hours given the time difference.

"What was all that about out there?" she asked Rory.

"There was someone watching us through binoculars. I spotted him when I caught the reflection on the lenses but couldn't see who it was."

"I'm surprised you noticed something like that."

Rory ignored her quip. "What aren't you telling me?"

Hannah sat silently by his desk. "This isn't the first time I have been followed. Yesterday when I met Scott in the bar he works in, someone followed me out. I gave him the slip and it may have been a coincidence but –"

"But?"

Hannah told him about the incident in St John's. "I'm

not in the habit of carrying bottles of gin in my bag and getting blind drunk during the day." She tried to make light of it but Rory could see how scared she'd been.

"I gave the bottle to DS Benton to have checked for fingerprints but nothing's come back."

"So you need to be extra careful." He stared at a fax that had just been passed to him. "You don't think this has anything to do with the dead Aussies, do you?"

"Who knows? I seem to have a knack for upsetting people."

"Oh Hannah what am I going to do with you? From now on keep me up to speed on all your meetings and interviews. And only take our account cars."

Hannah nodded. She'd also have to warn Janet.

Scott strolled over. "Right I've sent the email and included your contact details, Hannah, as it will be quicker that way. You have copies of everything now, so thanks for lunch. I'll be on my way."

Hannah walked with him to the lift. "Thanks for all your help, Scott. I passed your contact details to Leah but she asked me to give you her phone number." Hannah handed him a slip of paper. "She'd love to meet you."

"Thanks, I'll ring her."

"And take care, won't you?"

He laughed and shook her hand. "See you." The doors opened and shut and he and his wide smile were gone.

CHAPTER THIRTY-TWO

Elizabeth trotted in pushing her little doll's pram. The yellow and red plastic added a garish tone. She stopped in front of her mother. "Baby sick," she said. "We go to doctor."

"Oh poor baby." Hannah made a sad face. She wondered what was going on in her daughter's mind. Her visits to the GP were mercifully few.

"Shall I be doctor?" Hannah reached down from where she was sitting to pick up the patient.

"NO!" Elizabeth looked furious. "Doctor." And with that she marched out of the room leaving Hannah to wonder. It was time to visit Leah but just before she left the phone rang. DS Benton had found nothing at all on Colin Helmswood. Officially the man didn't exist. Hannah wondered why he had used an alias. Maybe he really did think he was at risk. But he hadn't really explained why apart from the fact that he had been placed with the Christian Brotherhood of the Holy Pilgrims. Nothing in his story added up

Hannah noticed a difference in her neighbour straightaway. There was a lightness she'd never seen before. Leah Braithwaite's smile was just as welcoming, but there was a radiance that lit up her face.

"I've spoken to him," she said.

"Who Scott?"

"No Adam." She led Hannah into her kitchen. This room was different too. It was as though it had been infused with happiness. Even the plants looked perkier. There was a pile of photos on the table beside the coffee pot. She beamed at Hannah. "He's my brother! Now it all makes sense."

"What does?" Hannah was intrigued.

Leah paused for a moment. "I know I was a deeply loved child. An only child. I had so many advantages and I have nothing to complain about. But there was always something missing. Something I couldn't understand. There were silences when I was growing up. Often I'd walk into a room and my parents would stop talking. They looked sad but they would smile and hug me. Sometimes I felt we lived with a ghost. And in a way we did although no one ever acknowledged it. The ghost of my brother who they thought had died. They must have felt ashamed for having left him at the foster home. I can see that now. I've been reliving moments; scenes in my life that now make sense. I used to blame myself but I wasn't culpable. None of us was."

She poured some coffee and cut some cherry cake. "My father's favourite," she explained with a smile. "My brother, Adam, sounds just like him. Obviously he has an Australian accent but the voice is essentially the same. I phoned early this morning so it was early evening for Adam." She smiled. The way she said his name lit a spark of joy in Hannah.

Her neighbour drank some coffee. "So what is Scott like?"

"I think you'll be proud of your nephew. A very determined, intelligent and sensitive young man who obviously adores his parents."

"My aunt Florrie said the same. I phoned her before I rang Adam. I was surprised she hadn't contacted me but maybe she didn't know how to broach the subject. She said he resembles my father." A smile played around her lips. "When I found these old photos after my mother died, I thought they must have been of my father. It didn't occur to me that... I never dreamed that I might have had a brother. And I have."

"I'm so pleased this has turned out so well for you."

Leah grasped her hand. There were tears in her eyes. "Thank you. Thank you. You don't know how much this means to me." She wiped her eyes with the back of her hand. "Sorry – I'm just over the moon."

Hannah left soon afterwards having learned that Leah had invited Scott to dinner. She would love to be a fly on the wall. As she let herself in to her own home she wondered what Leah's husband made of it all. In the meantime she had to change for her next appointment – one that was going to be far less enjoyable.

CHAPTER THIRTY-THREE

Funerals. There seemed no end to them. Hannah was furious with herself for agreeing to come. Harry Peters was nothing to her. She sat towards the back of the chapel, a good place to see everyone who was attending. She was wearing her hidden lapel camera. It went everywhere with her now. She scanned the pitiably few people present – Hannah wouldn't grace them with the term of mourners as she thought most were here for the food and drink afterwards – Lucy's old buddies from Cardboard City and Harry's drinking companions who hadn't noticed or hadn't been bothered that he hadn't been in the pub for several days. She glanced over to her right and saw DS Benton taking it all in. They had no clues about Harry's death – murder – but he was like a terrier not letting it go. Good for him she thought, knowing that it was his determined, plodding investigation that had saved her and the Kumars in May when they had been beaten and threatened by a gang who arranged for unwilling Asian brides to be disposed of. She smiled and he nodded.

It was then that she noticed him. Sherlock. Her whole body went into shock. Her arms felt leaden. Her stomach clenched and she had to concentrate on breathing deeply. Sherlock! This was the man who had taken a bullet meant for her on the steps of St John the Evangelist at Waterloo. He had placed himself in front of her and stood protecting her until... And then he disappeared. She had made enquiries but had never found him until she thought Mike the supply teacher at Linda's school was another incarnation. Then he too disappeared. Now here Sherlock was again. Undercover? He had a copy of *The Big Issue* in his hand and was stuffing it into his pocket. He nodded to a few of the Cardboard City dwellers then went to sit next to Lucy.

Next to Lucy. And she had asked Lucy time and again if she knew where he was. The liar! And after all she'd done for her. Hannah was torn between staying where she was, confronting the pair there and then, or just leaving. But if she left she'd never find out.

The service started. Hannah bowed her head not in prayer but in a determined effort to control her breathing and her temper. She'd been played. By a pair of vagrants. Bile rose in her throat. She swallowed. The priest said a few words. No eulogy. A recording of a hymn was played to avoid the embarrassment of no one singing or knowing the tune. The curtains swished to cover the coffin and the rumblings of the mechanism could be heard taking it to the furnace below. She shuddered. Memories of other, more personal, losses filled her mind.

A hand touched hers. "You okay luv?"

She thought she recognised the woman but through the blur of tears she couldn't be sure. She nodded and reached into her bag for a tissue. Blinking rapidly her eyes sought out Lucy and Sherlock. Lucy was being comforted by someone. Sherlock had disappeared. She blew her nose and went over to Mike Benton.

"Did you see where that guy who was sitting next to Lucy went?"

"He left a few moments ago with another man."

"You do know who he is, don't you?"

Benton eyed at her blankly.

"Sherlock!"

Benton was about to make a witty reply then thought the better of it. Hannah saw realisation dawn in his expression. "I'll pop outside and see if anyone saw where he went."

But they were too late. Hannah knew that. Sherlock was a man of many disguises like his fictional namesake. He was gone. But she wasn't going to let Lucy off the hook. Funeral or no funeral. Her fury meant she didn't see a man staring at her intently.

"So why didn't you tell me Sherlock was back?" Lucy was standing at the bar getting another round of drinks and Hannah pulled her arm so that she faced her.

"What're you drinking luv?" If Lucy thought she could deflect Hannah's questions she was seriously mistaken.

"I have a drink, thank you, but I want to know why you didn't tell me Sherlock was back?"

Lucy looked at her as though butter wouldn't melt. "You never asked me."

"But I did, Lucy. It was a while ago but you knew why I wanted to see him." Lucy stared at her showing no remorse. "To thank him – for saving my life." Hannah's temper was stretched to threadbare.

"I can't remember everything. I'm in mourning remember." Lucy was making the most of her grieving sister role, having dressed from head to toe in black.

Hannah knew it was useless to continue.

"Everything okay Lucy?" Edith had approached them.

She acknowledged Hannah with only a slight nod for which she was grateful.

"Yes thanks love." She patted Edith's hand. "Thanks so much for coming."

And don't thank me, Hannah thought. She finished her drink and left the pub. The wake, such as it was, could carry on without her. And Lucy could do one.

CHAPTER THIRTY-FOUR

Benton was no sooner at his desk than his phone rang and he was summoned to the boss's office.

"How was the funeral?" DI Claudia Turner asked pointing to a seat. "Coffee?"

"Thanks." She poured him a cup and one for herself. "Just a miserable funeral really."

Claudia stared at him. "Was Hannah there?"

"She was and none too happy to see 'Sherlock' appear at Lucy's side and then disappear before she could talk to him."

"Sensible man. Nothing else then?"

"No. Nothing to write home about. Anything else?" He'd finished his coffee.

His boss glanced down at a file on her desk. "Another Aussie death."

"You've got to be joking. Where this time?"

"Small B&B in Camberwell. Again, it looks like natural causes but…"

"But it's too much of a coincidence." Mike Benton hated coincidences at the best of times.

"Did you read the piece that Hannah wrote? She's made the connection that all these men – why only men? – could have been among those orphans who were sent out to Australia after the war. And hints that some of those were not orphans at all but were shipped out without their parents' knowledge or agreement."

"Christ. That's all we need."

"So why would someone want to get rid of them?"

"A cover-up?" Benton had read Hannah's article. He made a point of being up to speed with what the journalist was up to. Especially if it meant they might have to dig her out of some difficult situation.

"Could be. We need to check passenger lists into the UK for people who travelled from Australia within the last month. See if we can find some sort of link or…"

Mike groaned. "Needles in haystacks come to mind."

"I know but until we have anything concrete to go on. You can detail that to someone else tomorrow morning."

"Thanks."

Claudia smiled at his sour expression. "I've emailed Canberra to see if they've had a rash of unexplained deaths. Or anything they can help us with. We'll need to liaise re families of the deceased over there."

"And?"

"Still waiting." Claudia looked at her watch. "They should be waking up soon. But they won't reply straightaway. So you could pop over to Camberwell and see what the situation is there."

The bed and breakfast, a terraced house in a Camberwell side street, was modest but the owner was not. She was a stout woman with dyed ginger hair revealing an inch or so of grey roots and who spoke with an Irish accent you could slice cake with. Her feet were bare – and dirty – apart from the rings on her toes and her hands were large and – capable. Capable of what DS Benton wasn't sure but he did know he didn't want to get on the wrong side of Mrs O'Rourke. Everything about her was loud and he already had a headache. He paused his pen over the page in his notebook.

"So how long was it between seeing Bob Cardew check in and entering his room?"

"This morning. Everyone has to be out by 9am so the cleaner can get in. And some guests pay on a daily rate."

"Did Mr Cardew?"

"Did he what?"

"Pay daily for his room?" DS Benton could feel his patience, such that it was, slipping away.

"No, he paid for three weeks – cash in advance. He's only been here a week. Will I have to reimburse someone?"

Benton sighed. The poor sod was hardly cold.

"I won't be able to let it again until you lot are finished." She crossed her arms under her ample bosom. "And then I'll have the expense of an extra clean plus replacing the mattress and everything."

"I don't think we'll be much longer, Mrs O'Rourke, and I expect you'll be covered by your insurance." From her expression he guessed she had no insurance. He tapped his notebook. "So to your knowledge he didn't have any visitors?"

"No. I don't encourage visitors."

Benton thought it was a wonder she encouraged any guests. Except for the money.

He was about to put his notebook away and leave when she said, "It's a strange thing though. Someone else booked in for that night but didn't sleep in the bed. Must have left really early. Next room to your man."

"Was that a man or a woman?"

"Could be either. The name is Alex Landell," she said consulting the visitors' book.

"You didn't notice when he or she checked in?"

"Wasn't here. I left an envelope here with the key inside."

Benton looked confused. For someone who didn't allow guests to have visitors, she seemed remarkably cavalier about who came in and when.

"I can't be here twenty-four hours a day. I arranged to leave the key in a specific place."

"Okay, could you take me to the room?"

Mrs O'Rourke reached for a key on the shelf behind her and heaved herself off the chair. She squeezed herself out of the small office area. "Come on then."

He followed her up the narrow staircase and she paused at the door of a room adjacent to the crime scene. The paint was chipped and the number three hung precariously from one screw. Benton pulled out a pair of gloves and went in after the landlady unlocked the door. "Would you mind staying outside Mrs O'Rourke?" Her expression protested but she demurred.

The room was exactly like the one next to it that he'd visited earlier. Nothing seemed to have been touched. But there was something in the air. A slight odour he couldn't quite place. He opened the drawers of the night table and the wardrobe but no secrets were revealed.

As he was leaving he asked the scene of crime officers to dust the room for prints. It was a long shot but at least the DI wouldn't be able to say he hadn't been thorough.

CHAPTER THIRTY-FIVE

"So I have printouts of ships and the passenger lists for 1945 to 1960 which should cover the ages of the three men known so far to have died here recently."

"Where did you get all that?" Hannah was surprised to be interrupted by the young junior. She couldn't think why he had been included in the editorial meeting until she remembered he was the son of some friend of a friend of Lord Gyles.

"Public Records Office."

"Haven't you been busy?" The sneer in his voice made Hannah look up. She swallowed the sarcastic reply she was about to make. She'd come a long way from her early days freelancing for *The News* and she wasn't going to rise to the bait. But that young upstart would learn not to be so rude again.

"I've found two of our dead Aussies. They were both on a ship which left from Southampton in 1951. I need to find out what happened to them on arrival and where they went."

"Okay Miss Marple –"

That was the final straw. Hannah was about to respond when the editor, Georgina, cut in. "I think that's quite enough from you, Richard. When you have Hannah's experience and talent feel free to comment. Until then you're here to listen and learn." She glared at him. Maybe she was as fed up as everyone else with the proprietor's nepotism. "Excellent research Hannah. Perhaps you need someone to do some of the donkey work?"

Hannah was about to agree then saw where this was leading. No way did she want the uppity Mr Barret-Jones, muscling in on her territory.

"Having someone doing the photocopying and initial cross-checking would help. Richard you can work with Hannah on this."

It was an order. Hannah could feel herself flush but then looked across at Richard who seemed as though he was about to burst into tears. Interesting.

"Right, what other stories are we currently running with?"

The meeting ended soon after a brief discussion of where the Fred and Rose West case was heading. Rory joined Hannah. "Lunch?" She nodded gratefully. "Ten minutes?"

The brasserie was not too busy – most people were sitting outside in the sunshine so they managed to get a corner table inside. They both ordered from the set menu. "And to drink?" the waitress smiled vacantly.

"A bottle of house white, please." She took their menus and moved away.

"So what's happening in your world?"

Hannah stared across the room. "Not much if I'm honest. I feel as though my life is on hold."

"Because of Tom?"

"Partly. Mainly." The wine arrived; the waiter filled their glasses then moved away.

"You do seem to have lost some of your sparkle. Cheers."

"Thanks." Hannah drank some wine.

"Maybe it's some sort of post viral thing?"

"What?"

"The infection you had recently. Sometimes these viruses can leave you feeling really low."

"Well I need to snap out of it."

"You need to have some fun. That guy you were with at Lord Gyles's party seemed nice." Hannah had the distinct feeling she was being led into the conversation Rory wanted to have.

"He is. Well he seems to be. I don't really know that much about him except he's handy at deflecting glasses of wine thrown my way."

"Curious that."

"What his skill at deflecting wine glasses?"

"No that woman making such a scene. I couldn't make out who she was from the guest list."

Their food arrived and they ate in silence. "I did however see her talking with Mark at the beginning of the evening." There it was. Rory's goal.

"Did you?" Hannah's cutlery clattered to her plate. "How astonishing. Did they appear to know each other?"

Rory thought for a moment. "Yes they did."

Hannah pushed her plate away, her appetite gone. She drank some wine. "Do you think the wine incident was all a set-up?"

Rory studied her face. He didn't want to hurt her but she had to know. "It could have been. I don't know what their connection is but perhaps he was just trying to impress you."

Hannah skin felt clammy. "But why?"

"Maybe he fancies you." Hannah pulled a face. "Just be careful."

His mobile phone rang. He listened and signaled to the waitress for the bill. "Come on we're due back at the coalface."

As they walked back to the office, Hannah linked arms with Rory. "Thank you."

"For what – lunch?" He squeezed her arm.

"No for being a friend."

"Well you might not think that when you see what's landed on your desk."

Back at the office Hannah, saw a pile of printouts on her desk. One glance told her that Richard thought his work was done. Picking them up, she walked over to his desk. "Thank you for these, Richard. Now please check through them – meticulously – for the names and dates I gave you." His mouth opened as if to reply but seeing everyone in the office had turned to watch him, he nodded and Hannah strode back to her desk.

She checked her email. Then sent a short one to Adam asking if any of the people he had met up with had been sent to the Christian Brotherhood of the Holy Pilgrims. She needed some first hand information about what had been going on there.

Then she saw one email she had been waiting for. She read the contents, fired off a reply then picked up her bag and left. She decided not to use an account car and hailed a black cab on the main road.

The study was floor to ceiling bookshelves, and religious

icons; the windows were open on to a cloistered walkway enclosing a well-tended lawn and flower beds.

"Ms Weybridge, how do you do." The Right Reverend Joseph Mayhew, who had been sitting behind the huge mahogany desk, stood up and walked towards her, hand outstretched.

"How do you do, sir, and thank you for making the time to see me." The hand which gripped hers was warm and firm but Hannah noticed the skin on his hands was marked with dark brown age spots. His face looked stern in repose but his smile was encouraging.

"I was intrigued. How did you get the image you sent me?"

"A photographer working on a local residents project. I noticed the ring on someone's finger and had the image enlarged."

"I see. Please sit down. Would you like some tea?"

"No thank you but some water would be nice." The man picked up his phone and pressed a button. "Could we have some water, Miss Jackson? Thank you." He turned his attention back to Hannah. His deep blue eyes stared and she had the feeling he could read her thoughts.

"Have you seen this ring before?"

"I have. Once and I hoped to never see the like again." In the ensuing silence between them, Hannah could hear voices through the open window. She couldn't make out what was being said but it sounded as though two people were having an argument. "Some years ago, after the war, I was sent out to Australia to investigate an order of monks which seemed to have no allegiances or links to the established Catholic Church. Neither was The

Christian Brotherhood of the Holy Pilgrims affiliated to any Anglican or Protestant denomination. The monastery had been built in the middle of nowhere. Well not quite there was a small town within striking distance. Our information showed that children as young a six, sent out on the Child Migration Scheme had been allocated places there."

He paused as the door opened and Miss Jackson came in with a tray of iced water and glasses. She made no comment and left. The priest poured two glasses and handed one to Hannah.

"I had been told that the children had had to undergo gruelling physical labour to build the monastery. Rumour also had it that these children were abused mentally, spiritually and sexually." He sipped his water.

"The monks made me welcome after a fashion but contrived to avoid answering most of my questions. They were oblique about their finances but seemed to have reserves in gold and shares. In all I think there were only about ten resident monks. Most were older but there seemed to be one or two young men in training."

His expression was troubled. "There was an air of evil about the place. This may sound fanciful to you Ms Weybridge –"

"No, not at all, I –" The telephone ringing interrupted her.

"Miss Jackson I asked you to hold all calls." As he listened, his face betrayed nothing. "I see. Thank you." He turned his attention back to Hannah. "I'm sorry you were saying?"

"The idea of evil doesn't seem fanciful to me."

"No I don't suppose it does." He didn't elaborate but Hannah assumed he must know about her exposés even if he hadn't read them. "Anyway suffice it to say, I learned very little from my visit to the monastery. The Brotherhood made sure of that. Some time later I learned that the place had been set ablaze. It was thought at the time that some of the children who had been abused and tortured there – now men of course – returned. But who knows? God works in mysterious ways. Only a few of the monks escaped with their lives. All of the monks belonging to the Brotherhood wore the ring in the photograph."

That evening Mark arrived on her doorstep bearing a bouquet of flowers. Hannah's heart sank when she saw him via the security video camera.

"Sorry I took a chance that you'd be at home and apologies if I'm disturbing your evening." He looked harmless enough but could she trust him after what Rory had said. She took a gamble.

"Not at all, come in." She smiled as she stood aside for him to enter. It was a good thing he couldn't read her mind. She hated people turning up unannounced like this. It made her feel even more vulnerable. The fact that her hair was a mess and she had stains on her shirt from where Elizabeth had spat out her supper didn't help.

He followed her into the sitting room, still holding the flowers. "Look, I'm sorry I should have rung first but I didn't want to be fobbed off. I've come to apologise –" he handed her the flowers – "well, confess really."

Hannah sank onto one sofa. "Well sit down, then." Her abrupt tone brooked no dissent.

Mark sat on the other sofa. "I'm leaving tomorrow. Back to Bosnia."

"Right."

"So I didn't want to leave without... I told you a lie. Well a lie by omission."

Hannah said nothing.

"I know the woman who threw the wine at you at Lord Gyles' reception. She's a friend of my wife's." Hannah's expression didn't change. "We're separated. Not divorced because if anything happened to me while on active service she'd be much better off financially. Anyway that woman confronted me before we sat down to eat. Thought I should be back with Jane, which is a laugh as she tried it on with me a few months before we split up. Her husband stepped in and apologised." He took a deep breath. Hannah's silence wasn't making it easier for him. "They must have argued and the rest you know. She's a bitter woman. But I wanted you to know that it had nothing to do with you. In case you had been worried about..."

His voice tailed off. At least Hannah could rest easy on that count. "Well, thanks for telling me."

"You don't seem surprised."

"No." Rory had been right but she wasn't going to tell Mark that. "Would you like a glass of wine?"

They took their wine and sat in the garden. The evening was still warm and somewhere a neighbour was having a barbeque. The smell of charcoal and burning meat wafted over.

"Thank you for the flowers. I'm not usually so surly but it's been a long day."

Mark looked around the garden – the sandpit, the doll's pram and tea set all evidence of the younger resident. "It can't be easy bringing up a child on your own."

"I'm lucky – I can afford a nanny and she's brilliant."

"Yes James told me."

"Have you seen much of him lately?"

"Hardly at all – he works all hours, as you know. And tomorrow I'm off for another tour of duty." He smiled. "Perhaps on my next leave we could have that meal together."

"That would be nice." No one seeing her smile would have guessed Hannah was actually wondering when and if Tom would ever contact her.

Mark finished his drink and stood up. "Thanks for the wine. I must be off as I have an early start tomorrow."

At the front door Mark stooped to kiss her on the cheek. "Take care, Hannah."

"You too." She watched him walk away from the house and closed the door. At least that was one mystery solved. And, for once, it didn't have anything to do with her. She smiled at the thought of being a 'scarlet woman' and went to bed that night with a less heavy heart.

CHAPTER THIRTY-SIX

Hannah was thinking about the murders of the Australian men, which according to the police were not violent attacks. In fact the victims apparently looked peaceful. Who would do this? And why? The phone rang.

"Hi Hannah, I've managed to get some information you asked me for." Joe's voice sounded as though he was speaking under water.

"Where are you? You sound strange."

"I'm using a new mobile. The signal's a bit weak. But I've found someone who has some classified information to pass on to you."

Hannah had wondered why she hadn't heard from Joe. Apparently his friend in Manchester hadn't been very informative. It was good to know he hadn't forgotten. "Okay."

"It's all a bit cloak and dagger. You need to be at the National Portrait Gallery in an hour's time. Can you manage that?"

Hannah glanced at her watch. "Just about. Why the rush?"

"No idea. But you need to sit on the bench in front of the large portrait of Queen Elizabeth I in Room 2." He told her how the contact would address her and how she was to reply.

"Right well I'd better be on my way then."

Joe rang off. Hannah collected her briefcase and rang for a minicab – she couldn't rely on *The News* account cars getting to her in time.

As instructed she sat on the bench in the middle of the room, studying "The Coronation Portrait" of Queen Elizabeth I. It was cool in here. Outside the heat was draining. What must it have been like to have worn those heavy and uncomfortable gowns with constricting corsets underneath? Her own cotton frock looked like an undergarment in comparison.

Someone sat down beside her. Her peripheral vision took in a dark haired man in a light linen suit.

"One of my favourite paintings," he said without turning towards her. "I always take a few moments in front of the Virgin Queen whenever I'm here." That had been the introduction she was listening for.

"I admire the way the light falls on her face," was her rejoinder. She felt the movement beside her but resisted the urge to look. To all intents and purposes she was totally engrossed in the painting of Elizabeth's coronation. She waited a few moments.

"I'll leave you to your ruminations." Hannah half-smiled as she picked up the newspaper he had placed between them and put it in her bag. She had felt his touch. She stood up and moved to the next room, slowly walking round and admiring the various portraits of the Plantagenets.

By the time she made her way back to Room 2, past Elizabeth whose enigmatic haughty expression matched the regality of her posture, the man had gone. She smiled at the memory of him and wondered who he was. No names had been mentioned. And no clue as to why he was passing on sensitive, confidential information.

•

Hannah made sure the envelope that had been inside the newspaper was secure in her brief case. A copy of *The Daily Telegraph* dated a week ago. She wondered if that had any relevance. She could check the date at *The News* offices for anything in the political diary.

She hailed a taxi on Charing Cross Road. It gave her time and space to think but in fact she found the heat and the sound of the engine had a soporific effect on her. They were going over Westminster Bridge when her mobile rang.

She listened to the voice at the other end in silence then leaned forward and tapped the glass inside the cab. "Change of direction if you don't mind." She gave him the new address and sat back as they turned left into York Road and made their way eastwards.

Rory walked towards her beaming. She was sitting in The Ship on Borough High Street, their 'secret rendez-vous' venue. He had been at the bar when she entered so she sat at a corner table and waited. By the way he grinned at her when she came in, whatever he had to say was good news.

"So what did I tell you?" He placed a bottle of champagne and two glasses on the table.

"About what?" Hannah watched the bubbles crescendo to the top of the glass as he poured.

"About our would-be novelist Judy Barton."

"That she has a publishing deal with Hallstone Books?"

Rory was still wearing his Cheshire Cat expression.

"Exactly. And who did I say had a major share holding?"

"Lord Gyles." Hannah found these silly questions tiresome.

"And who has just had her book pulled indefinitely?"

Hannah's look of incredulity made Rory laugh as he handed her a glass of Champagne. "To friends in high places!"

"But she had a publishing deal. If they pull the book she'll just take it elsewhere."

Rory was shaking his head. "She didn't read the small print. Hallstone Books bought all rights for seven years and they only have to publish within that time. She has to wait seven years before she can offer it to another publisher."

Hannah could feel her body relax from her shoulders down. It was as though the Champagne was coursing through her body, each bubble exploding a pinprick of tension. It was only when Rory handed her a tissue that she realised she was crying.

"Hey this is a celebration not a wake."

"I know." She sniffed loudly. "I'm just so relieved and … and thankful."

"Good. Here's the fish and chips I ordered." He smiled at the barman who had brought over two plates.

Hannah hadn't realised how hungry she was and the fish and chips seemed like the best she'd ever tasted. And the Champagne certainly helped. Her mood had scaled up to euphoric.

"So how's the investigation into the deaths of these Aussies going?" Rory asked when they'd finished eating.

Hannah smiled remembering where she'd been

returning from when Rory had called her. She was itching to check out what had been passed to her.

"Not sure, but I think it's beginning to come together. I just need to check a few more things."

"Keep me in the loop, won't you?" Rory looked concerned. "Don't put yourself at risk in any way at all."

Hannah laughed. "As if."

But her attitude was exactly what Rory was afraid of.

CHAPTER THIRTY-SEVEN

The copies of the memos had been heavily redacted. Key names had been obliterated as had some of the dates. However Hannah could see that the correspondence between key government offices in Canberra and London was outlining a way to cover up and stop speculation about the exploitation and mistreatment of children sent out to Australia after the war. There were allegations of physical and sexual abuse perpetrated by members of some religious institutions where British children had been placed as part of the migration scheme.

So far she knew that Jeff Collins who had died in Dulwich Library and Len Smarley who died in Manchester had been in one of those institutions. Had someone been sent to stop them from making allegations? It seemed unlikely as they had been looking for members of their biological families. But the social worker in Nottingham had been making a lot of noise about the Child Migration Scheme. Maybe people were trying to cover up the worst cases.

Hannah had tried to research the Christian Brotherhood of the Holy Pilgrims but had found very little except confirmation of what Bishop Mayhew had told her – that it had been disbanded if that was the right word in the seventies after a major fire. A fire. How convenient. Especially if governments were involved in a cover up about what had happened to the children.

And there had been two other deaths. Francis Jones in Burgess Park and Bob Cardew in a B&B in Camberwell.

A coincidence? Or had they all been part of the Child Migration Scheme?

"It was my sixth birthday. A date I would never be able to celebrate again. That was the day I arrived at the so-called monastery. It was nothing but a small wooden chapel with various outbuildings. A monk led me to a dormitory with camp beds for about twenty boys. He pushed me towards one and told me to strip off my clothes. I was all fingers and thumbs and had trouble with some of the buttons. Out of nowhere a belt thrashed me across my buttocks – the buckle end of the belt. I screamed and was thrashed again. My dad hit me once. Across my calves. It hurt. But not like this. The pain was terrible. As I stood there sniveling I wet myself..."

Tears poured down Hannah's face as she read the account that had come within another, sealed envelope. Written across the top in red was "Just the tip of the iceberg".

This was a transcript of an interview with a man who had suffered terrible physical and sexual abuse at the hands of members of a religious sect, which seemed to have no direct links with the Vatican or any other organised religion. As if the torment of hard physical labour for the children – some as young as six years old – wasn't enough for them to contend with, there was the horrific sexual abuse. Some were so badly injured they died. Some took their own lives. Some, like the interviewee, eventually managed to escape only to find they were not believed when they thought they'd found a refuge. *"I learned not to cry. I felt if I started I would never be able to stop."*

Nothing in the memos – or nothing that she could see – linked to The Christian Brotherhood of the Holy Pilgrims. Hannah pondered on how she could best use this information and decided to run the name of the Brotherhood past the deputy editor. Plus the information she'd had from the Right Reverend Joseph Mayhew. Was the person in Edith's photos wearing the ring connected in some way to the Brotherhood? The thought made her blood run cold.

The phone rang and before she could even say her name Judy's voice screeched at her. "You fucking bitch. You've got what you wanted so why did you have to screw up my life as well? What possible pleasure can it give you to ruin my chances of…"

"Hey hold on Judy…"

"Don't tell me to hold on, you smug cow."

"Judy, if you're talking about your book being withdrawn, I assure you that had nothing to do with me."

"Oh no, then how come you know about it then?"

"Rory told me."

"Rory? What the fuck has he got to do with anything?"

"Judy calm down." She could hear Judy trying to control her breathing. "Did you know that Lord Gyles is a major shareholder in Hallstone Books?"

"Oh shit! Trust my fucking luck." There was an ominous silence. Then what sounded like a sob.

"Judy this really had nothing to do with me."

"If you say so. But you appear to be his lordship's pet Polly Pocket at the moment."

Hannah failed to see the relevance of that remark and let it go. "Judy I..." There was no point in continuing as the line went dead.

Hannah felt a prickle of fear. Judy wasn't someone to cross as she had previously discovered and the last thing she needed was some other nasty surprise.

CHAPTER THIRTY-EIGHT

How many weeks had it been since their holiday and she still hadn't heard from Tom? Claudia knew nothing. Joe hadn't been able to find out anything either. It was almost as though he no longer existed. Maybe that was the plan, she thought.

Then there was the time in the pub with Lucy when she thought she'd seen him. But like an apparition he'd disappeared into thin air. If he had been there at all. The mind plays tricks; such a deceiving attribute. She thought Tom would have let her know in some way. Or would he? Maybe he was following orders to ignore her?

Working helped but her emotional life was on hold and that was something she needed to sort. Family life needed an injection of fun. For Elizabeth's sake if not her own.

"Have you planned any holiday?" she asked Janet that morning as she cleared the breakfast table. Elizabeth was busy drawing a picture.

"No. I usually avoid the school holidays when the prices are higher. I was thinking of going to visit my friend Rosa who lives in a small town on the Costa Brava in September although I was going to clear it with you first."

"I haven't made any plans but it would make sense for me to take time off when you're away. I should take this little minx to see her grandparents." There was a moment's silence between the women. Both thinking about their respective mothers. "Will your sister come and stay with your mother while you're away?"

"Yes – at least I hope so. She usually does although she can be unpredictable. But if not Mum will stay with her sister in Brentwood."

"Right, so why don't you book your flights and I'll arrange our trip for the same time?"

It felt good to be planning. To be looking forward. Even if that future did not involve or include Tom. Even the image she had of him was beginning to fade. The features bleached out. The character blurring. The timbre of his voice quietening. Could their relationship such that it was, survive this separation?

Hannah stared at her computer screen. Her reflection scolded her. She should concentrate on her daughter's happiness. It was time to get ready for her trip to Blackwater House. She booked her cab to Waterloo Station and packed her briefcase. She'd already told Rory about her visit. Then she thought about letting DI Turner know.

Her call went straight through to answerphone so she left a message. She would be back by the evening.

Sitting on the train, Hannah considered the possibilities that Blackwater House might offer. From her research, she knew the house had been closed up since the late sixties and there seemed to be some confusion as to who now owned it. So she had concentrated on the church that stood in the grounds next to it and had made an appointment to see the current incumbent, the Reverend Ian Joyce, who had seemed happy to talk with her on the phone. He had sounded welcoming when she told him of her proposed visit. No sense of any cover-up there.

She wondered, not for the first time, if she was on a wild goose chase but if nothing else she'd see the place for herself, take some photographs and examine the headstones in the cemetery.

Hannah was relieved to see a taxi office outside the station and managed to get a cab straightaway to St Anne's vicarage.

"On the way could you drive past Blackwater House, if possible?"

The driver nodded. "I can but there's not much to see. The house is set back in the grounds and the gates have been chained up since they closed the orphanage down."

The driver appeared to be in his mid-fifties. "Have you always lived here?"

"Born and bred. I was only a nipper when Blackwater House was an orphanage. Played there sometimes. But kids didn't stay there long... so you couldn't make proper friends." He changed gear and the car slowed.

"Here we are, coming up on your left... Blackwater House." He pulled into the side of the road so his passenger could get a better view.

Hannah got out of the car but could hardly make out the actual building. Trees and shrubs obscured her vision and the huge black wrought iron gates were indeed locked and chained. They made her think of Sleeping Beauty's castle as she'd been reading the story to Elizabeth.

"I wonder someone doesn't bulldoze it down. Get rid of all those ghosts," the driver said once she was back in the cab.

"Ghosts?" Hannah was intrigued.

"I don't mean real ones – although there could be, I suppose – but it's like the past haunts it. Won't let it go. All potential sales fall through." He started the car again and a few minutes later turned left and drove into the church grounds. The church, weatherworn and squat with high, dark red doors and a bell tower to one side, stood between Blackwater House and the vicarage. "That'll be £3.20 and here's my card in case you need a taxi back."

"Thanks." Hannah handed him £5. "Keep the change. But could I have a receipt?" The driver handed her a blank receipt. She got out of the car as a man in clerical black approached her. He held out his hand. "You must be Hannah, welcome. I'm Ian Joyce." His smile was warm, disarming. "Let's go into the vicarage. I expect you could do with a coffee."

The vicar led her through a sunny hall into an even brighter study. Where the walls were not lined with bookshelves, they were adorned with religious pictures and icons. A huge depiction of Saint Anne with her daughter the Virgin Mary held centre stage. Hannah stood in front of it contemplating whether it was a print of a famous work or an original by a minor artist. Either way she didn't much care for it.

"She's the patron saint of unmarried women, housewives, women in labour or who want to be pregnant, grandmothers and, of course, your name Saint whose festival day is today 26 July. Such a coincidence, don't you think?"

So quietly had the priest come into the room with a tray of coffee and biscuits that Hannah had jumped.

"Sorry I startled you. Do sit down."

Hannah sank into a comfy sofa. Through the open latticed windows the songs of birds competed with the church bell ringing the hour. Midday.

"I thought we could have a wander over to the House after coffee then come back for some lunch."

"That's very kind of you." She drank some coffee. "But I thought the house was all locked up."

"It is. But there's access through the churchyard and I have a key." He smiled at Hannah's surprise. "Apparently it was given to one of the previous incumbents who didn't see fit to return it when the orphanage closed down. Since then it's been passed on to each vicar. My legacy so to speak."

They finished their coffee and Hannah noticed that the priest had put something into a leather satchel that he slipped over his shoulder as they walked out into the garden, which was a riot of summer flowers in bloom and mature fruit trees. Further to the left Hannah could see a well-tended vegetable garden. Just for a moment she closed her eyes and inhaled the heady perfumes of an English garden in summer. And freesia. That scent brought a smile to her face.

The vicar had walked ahead and opened the gate into the church cemetery. Hannah caught up with him. "Some of these graves date back many centuries. But those over there are more recent. Most just before the end of or just after the Second World War. Children mainly."

His expression was grim. "There was never really a proper investigation after the fire."

"The fire?"

"Yes, apparently it started in the office where all the records were kept. Rather convenient given what the staff were being accused of."

"Which was?"

"Faking deaths and sending children off on the Child Migration Scheme without parental consent. Also some children seemed to have died very young – according to the gravestones. And there were all sorts of rumours at the time, according to my older parishioners."

They'd reached an overgrown hedge. Pushing aside some branches to reveal a gate, the priest produced the key and the hinges growled in protest as he pulled the gate open. It was like entering the Secret Garden. Everything was overgrown. Weeds had won dominion. Much was scorched from this unusually hot summer. Away from the main building was a hotchpotch of outhouses in varying states of disrepair.

Ian led Hannah along a barely discernable path to some French windows. He inserted another key and the door opened with barely a creak. As he walked in, the priest made a sign of the cross and then stopped, like a tracker dog, nose in air. "That's strange."

"What is?"

"There's a smell of incense."

Hannah thought of the "haunting" that the cab driver had described. It was darker and much cooler in the house and she felt a frisson of fear as though the walls had absorbed the terrible history of the house.

"Someone's been in here." The priest's voice was barely above a whisper.

"How can you tell? Does anyone else have keys?"

"No idea about the keys but I come in here from time to time just to check up on things." Hannah wondered what he checked up on as he continued, "Look you can see where the dust has been disturbed when that chair was moved."

Hannah took a photograph and then some general shots of the room. They went through another door and along a corridor, which Hannah noticed had blackened walls. "The fire was in here." The priest opened the door. Again he made the sign of a cross: "In the name of the Father and the Son and the Holy Spirit." Hannah noticed he sprinkled some liquid from a small phial.

"What's that for?"

"Holy water. To bless whatever spirits may reside here." He smiled at Hannah's expression of disbelief. "Belt and braces," he said. "Being prepared."

They both stared at the room in silence. Maybe she was being fanciful but Hannah thought there was still a whiff of smoke in the air; it was quite obvious that all the records would have been destroyed in the fire. However it seemed amazing that the fire could have been so effective in here without spreading to the whole house.

"Is it safe to walk around the rest of the building?"

"Yes, the fire was contained here – obviously arson – and there was no structural damage. It seems the fire brigade was alerted fairly quickly. But too late for this room." Hannah was amused at the expression on his face. A mixture of disbelief and controlled fury.

Walking down another corridor into the main entrance hall, Hannah was overwhelmed by sadness. She could almost hear the sobs echoing back over the years. And yet presumably before it became an orphanage there had been a family in the manor house. Perhaps they hadn't been happy either. The ground floor rooms were soulless and what little furniture they contained was mostly covered in grubby sheets but Hannah could imagine a different scenario.

"I'm surprised no one has bought the place and renovated it. It looks as though it would have been magnificent in its day."

"It was. I have some old photos back at the vicarage. There have been prospective buyers but something always happens to put them off." He didn't elaborate. They climbed the staircase. There was a noise. Ian's hand stopped her moving forwards. The noise again. He put his finger to his lips and they continued upstairs as quietly as they possibly could on an old, uncarpeted, wooden staircase that creaked and moaned as if in protest at being disturbed. At the top the vicar opened a door straight ahead. He again made a sign of the cross, mouthed some silent words and entered. Another bang and Hannah almost jumped out of her skin. The priest moved forward and shut an open window that had caused the noise. He sniffed the air and Hannah too could smell the incense.

"Someone has been staying here."

"How can you be sure?" The room to Hannah's eyes looked as though it hadn't been occupied since presumably the last of the children had left. But then she noticed a table, which had been cleaned where everything else in the dormitory was covered with cobwebs and dust.

"Perhaps a homeless person...?"

"Perhaps. But a homeless person with a penchant for incense?" The priest face betrayed his scepticism.

Hannah took more photos especially of the walls by the beds where there were faded drawings and names scratched onto the wallpaper. One bed, however, had recently been slept on and the wall behind it had been scrubbed clean.

Ian looked seriously troubled when she pointed this out to him.

"Something is not right here." At the door he turned and blessed the room; they crossed the corridor to another door, which opened into another dormitory the mirror of the one they had just been in. Nothing seemed to have been disturbed here.

The vicar blessed the room. "If you've seen enough?"

Hannah took a few more photos and they left the house to its secrets and heartache.

CHAPTER THIRTY-NINE

Hannah was glad to be outside in the fresh air and sunshine again. The priest said another prayer before locking the door. As he turned towards her she could see that his expression was troubled and his smile was forced. He led her back through the grounds to the gate in the wall into the churchyard and the children's gravestones. They were remarkably well tended in comparison to most of the others.

Ian answered her unspoken question. "Someone set up a trust fund leaving money to make sure these graves were always cared for. I believe it was one of the parents who lost a child."

Hannah photographed each stone. She was searching for one name in particular but Edward Peters did not feature among the buried.

"So what has brought you here, Hannah?" The priest asked as she stood by the last gravestone.

She put her camera away. "A combination of factors, really. One person has asked me to try and trace her cousin. There's also a possibility that another family I know lost a child here. Plus," she hesitated. It sounded farfetched.

"Plus?"

She looked into his eyes. Was his concern a practised reaction he'd learned in his job? "Plus there have been several murders in London which seem to be linked in some way to the Child Migration Scheme."

They had reached the vicarage and he stood aside for

her to enter.

"And to Blackwater House?"

"That I don't know but Blackwater House has cropped up a few times in my research and all of the victims had returned to the UK to try and trace their families or what remained of them."

"Understandable that they should look for their families but why would anyone kill them?"

Hannah didn't reply. The answers were beginning to stack up but she wasn't in a position to share those. She followed him into the kitchen.

"Home made bread, cheese and salad. Okay for you?"

"That would be lovely, thank you. Is there anything I can do?"

"You could lay the table. Cutlery in that drawer over there. He had his back to her, retrieving food from the fridge. She opened a drawer and staring up at her was a clipping of her article in *The News* about the dead Australians. Realising her mistake she closed it quietly and opened its neighbour for the cutlery. But she couldn't help wondering why the vicar had kept that cutting without acknowledging it to her.

Ian said a short grace and, as they sat to eat lunch, Hannah asked, "How long have you been vicar here?"

He broke off some bread. "Nearly seven years. My first parish after my curacy."

Hannah thought he looked older than that timeframe would have suggested. Ian seemed good at mindreading. "I trained as a teacher first and taught maths for a few years before I found my true vocation." He filled her glass. "Home made lemonade." Again he read her mind. "No I didn't make it; it's a gift from one of my churchwardens. And it's delicious."

It was – perfect for a hot, summer's day.

"Do you have a special reason for visiting Blackwater House?"

"I found the name in an address book belonging to someone who had died. It seemed that her son may have been sent here. Maybe died here."

Ian finished eating. "We do have some records here. Of the burials. Or those that were known about. I've been checking through the records – someone else was asking me about the children." He stood up abruptly not elaborating on who had asked him. "Come with me."

Hannah followed him into the church. It seemed larger inside than it had appeared from the outside and it everything about it gleamed. A building that was loved and cared for. Ian genuflected before the altar and opened a large black wooden door to one side, which led to a narrow corridor and another door. "This is the Sacristy. We keep all our records here."

Hannah must have revealed her shock. "Only copies. The originals are filed at Church House."

Nevertheless they were kept in a large safe that looked as though it had been rooted there for generations, cemented into the floor. He opened the safe and removed one book. "I left it on the top in case you wanted to see it." He placed the book on the desk and invited Hannah to sit. "I'll leave you for a short while if you don't mind as I have to see someone at the vicarage. Call through on that phone when you've finished."

•

Hannah found nothing – at least no names that interested her in the deaths registered between 1944 and 1955 but she took a few photographs of the pages. On a whim she scanned down the column devoted to baptisms. And bingo! there he was Edward Peters. So either he was sent away on the Child Migration Scheme or … or he could have been placed in care elsewhere, or adopted or died later.

She could ask Claudia if she would run his name through the police databases. She wondered if *The News* could facilitate access to National Insurance records. It would save time if she rang Rory now. She took out her mobile phone. No signal. She picked up the phone on the Sacristy desk and pressed the button for the vicarage. It rang and rang…

She hung up and considered at the numbers on the side of the phone. Nine for an external line. She dialled Rory's number. The voice of one of the subs greeted her.

"Sorry, Rory isn't available at the moment."

Hannah's fingers tapped the wooden desk in irritation. "Do you know how long he'll be? It's Hannah Weybridge."

"Oh hi Hannah. They're all in a meeting. There was a car bomb explosion outside the Israeli Embassy."

"Christ, when was that?"

"Just after midday. Everyone's tied up with that at the moment."

"Of course. Did anyone die?"

"No mainly cuts and bruises. Apparently it was a woman in a car with false number plates."

"Okay, thanks I'll catch up later."

Hannah was appalled by what had happened but at least there were no fatalities. But there could be repercussions. She was unlikely to get anything from the office today. She really needed to be leaving soon. She tried ringing the vicarage again, but no reply. As she replaced the receiver she thought she saw a shadow pass by the open door.

"Hi Ian – I've been trying to call you."

No one answered. She looked around for a safe place to conceal the ledger. The only possibility was under a pile of folded altar cloths. Without turning she sensed rather than heard a presence behind her. The hairs on the back of her neck tingled. She bent down to pick up her bag as though to leave and glanced between her legs. A shadow faded away …

Her footsteps echoed as she walked through the church. Every few steps she stopped and listened. Nothing. Her imagination was in overdrive. Outside the church was preternaturally quiet. No birds. No cars passing on the road. The stillness was unsettling. She turned to see Blackwater House silhouetted against the vivid blue sky. Was it fanciful to think of a building as evil? Someone had been there. Was that person looking for what she hoped to discover?

Hannah let herself into the vicarage by the kitchen door. "Ian?" There was no answer. "Hello? Ian?"

There was a muffled sound from the priest's study. Hannah opened the door and froze. The vicar was sitting on the floor, holding a handkerchief to the side of his head. It was covered with blood. Hannah stared in horror until the ringing of the telephone made her spring into action. She ignored it and knelt beside Ian. "What happened? Shall I call an ambulance or the police?"

"No I..." Ian struggled to stand.

Hannah helped him up and sat him in an armchair.

"Vicar?" the voice got louder. "The front door was open so... Oh heavens!" The man who came through the door looked aghast. "I saw someone disappearing around the back of the church. Someone in a hurry so thought I'd check. Well it's a good job I did."

The man, who, it transpired, was one of the churchwardens called John, immediately took charge of the situation and phoned the police and an ambulance even though the vicar protested it wasn't necessary.

Hannah had a horrible thought. "Ian I'm so sorry I left that register in the Sacristy. Shall I check it's still there?"

John answered. "I'll go. Where did you leave it?"

"Under a pile of altar cloths." She decided not to mention the shadow she'd seen. If that person had taken the book there was little she could do about it.

Within minutes John returned. "It's gone." Surprisingly he didn't look angry. "Don't worry Hannah it's only a copy." He smiled at her and the vicar. "And I have my own copy too."

Some colour had returned to Ian's face. "I wonder if our intruder and thief are one and the same person? Perhaps looking for answers as you are, Hannah?"

"Perhaps." Hannah checked the time. She felt guilty

leaving them but she had a train to catch.

Ian anticipated her. "John, would you mind running Hannah to the station?"

"Oh there's no need. I'll get a taxi."

"It's no trouble." John took some keys from the desk. "I'll be back soon Ian. Joan will be across in a moment or two."

Hannah shook Ian's hand. "Will you phone me later when you feel better?" She gave him her card and he nodded.

"God be with you, Hannah."

John was quiet as he drove her to the station but Hannah didn't feel it was an unfriendly silence. More shyness. "Do you know who Ian was seeing this afternoon, John?"

"No one as far as I know. Except you. Why?"

"When he left me in the Sacristy he said he had to see someone."

"Something must have come up. People bring their problems. He's a good man and generous with his time."

"Certainly he was generous with it to me." Hannah smiled.

"Yes." John changed gear and slowed down as they approached the station. "Time to let sleeping dogs lie, I think."

"I'm sorry?"

"No need to dig up the past of that place. It won't bring any one of those poor children back will it?"

"But supposing some of them are coming back to find their families?"

John stopped the car. "Good luck to them."

"And if they are being killed?" John looked horrified. Hannah got out of the car. "Thanks for the lift." She made the London train with minutes to spare.

The compartment was almost full but she found a seat at a table facing the way they were travelling. She felt hot and sticky and upset by the assault on Ian Joyce. Assuming that the person who attacked him was the same one who had spent at least one night at Blackwater House, was that person also responsible for the murders? Hannah looked down the carriage and saw a priest sitting a few rows down facing her. He was wearing heavy, black-rimmed glasses so it was impossible to see much of his face. She smiled tentatively but there was no response. At the next station the priest alighted from the train and Hannah returned to her thoughts so she didn't see him enter the next carriage along.

CHAPTER FORTY

The next day Hannah was at her desk early, organising her notes and impressions of Blackwater House. The interruption of the telephone ringing was not welcome.

"Hi Hannah. Mike Benton."

She was surprised he was calling her. Usually it was Claudia who kept in touch. "To what do I owe this pleasure?"

"You gave me that gin bottle…"

"Oh yes – any luck?"

"Not sure. Ordinarily you'd expect quite a lot of prints, packer, shopkeeper and so on but this one had been wiped clean – almost."

Hannah wondered where this was leading.

"We lifted a couple of prints but nothing came up in our automated system."

"Ye-es."

The excitement in his voice was palpable. "We've just come up with a match."

Hannah's stomach clenched. "And?"

"And you're not going to like this – the print matches a partial we found at that B&B in Camberwell." Silence. "Are you still there, Hannah?"

"I am." Her voice was small. Afraid. "Mike I think I've been followed a few times. Not all the time obviously but…"

"Shit Hannah why didn't you mention it?"

"I thought I was overreacting."

"Right stay where you are and I'll send someone over

to bring you to the station to make a full statement." With that he rang off.

Hannah wrote a note for Janet. Picked up her bag and waited downstairs. She saw the police car park outside and watched a young woman officer get out and come to the door which Hannah opened before the bell was rung.

"Ms Weybridge? I'm PC Sheridan James." She held up her warrant card. "Sergeant Benton sent me to collect you." Her Welsh lilt and warm smile calmed Hannah and made her feel ridiculous for feeling so scared just a few minutes before.

"Thank you." She switched on the alarm and locked the door behind them.

Leah was walking up the street towards her. "Everything all right, Hannah?"

"Yes thanks. I'll call you later if that's okay."

Leah nodded and crossed the road to her own house.

Hannah smiled at her driver. Another ride in a police car. Her neighbours must love her.

The interview room, just off the entrance to the station, was uncomfortable and smelled of other people's sweat and fear.

PC James was sitting in on the interview. She had remained mercifully quiet during their short journey. However as they parked she said, "I really admire your investigations for *The News*."

"Thank you." Hannah smiled.

"But don't you ever get scared?"

Memories of her fear were embedded in her bones now. "I do but usually it makes me more careful. And I remind myself that other people don't have the protection I enjoy."

DS Benton had been waiting for them. "Right let's start at the beginning. When were you first aware of being followed?"

"I'm not sure really. It was just a feeling at first and I thought I was overreacting, imagining things."

Mike nodded. "But you weren't."

"It seems not. Outside Lucy Peters' block of flats, I had the impression someone was watching me. Obviously the incident at St John's, Waterloo."

"And you didn't see your assailant there?"

"No. I heard a voice say something but I can't remember what. Then someone followed me out of The George pub in Soho where Scott Baylis is working."

"Scott Baylis?"

"He's a young Aussie. It turns out he's my neighbour's nephew. His father was shipped away on the Child Migration Scheme."

Benton nodded. "Go on."

"Then Rory – the news editor," she added before Benton could ask – "thought he saw someone spying on us with binoculars when we took Scott out for lunch."

"Do you have a contact number for this young man?"

Hannah took out her Filofax. PC James passed her a piece of paper and she wrote down the telephone numbers and address Scott had given her. The young woman left the room.

"Anything else you need to tell me?" Benton's tone belied his irritation. Trust Hannah to be holding back.

Hannah looked uncomfortable. She stared at her

hands. "I've received some sensitive information."

"From?"

"I can't say."

"For Christ's sake Hannah – help us out here."

"I can't say because I don't know. I was put in touch with someone who delivered the information."

"Who put you in touch?"

Hannah stared at him, wide-eyed. She scratched her hand. "I can't tell you that either. That person would be vulnerable."

"So what did the information concern?" It was like getting the proverbial blood from a stone.

"It was highly confidential." Hannah looked more and more uncomfortable. "It concerns a cover up by two governments."

Benton groaned. "You never do things by halves do you."

PC James came back into the room. Benton and Hannah stared at her flushed face. "Scott Baylis has left his job and where he was staying. But apparently the house where he had a room had been broken into and his room ransacked. The person I spoke to wasn't sure about the timing."

Hannah could feel the room spinning. What was she going to tell Leah? How was she going to tell her? She sipped the water she'd been given earlier. Her mobile rang. "Would you mind if I answer this?" Benton nodded and both officers left the room.

She listened as the Reverend Ian Joyce told her that the police had found just one or two fingerprints of interest in Blackwater House. "No doubt the police will be in touch with you. But apparently they are a match for a case in London."

Hannah allowed the implications to settle. "Thank you Ian. Are you okay?"

"Yes, no lasting damage. But you must be careful."

"I will. By the way who were you meeting when you were attacked?"

"A parishioner but he didn't turn up. When I went into my study I surprised someone searching through my desk. He hit me with a paperweight and you know the rest."

"So you didn't get a good look at him?"

"No not really but…"

"But?"

"He was wearing a clerical collar."

"A priest?" Hannah's voice betrayed her incredulity.

"Not necessarily. It's a good disguise in a church."

"I suppose it is. Thanks Ian I'll let you know what happens."

Benton and James returned with coffees as she ended the call. Four coffees. DI Turner followed them in. "Hello Hannah. There's been a development with the fingerprint. Same one turned up at Blackwater House."

"I know. The vicar there just phoned to tell me. He was attacked by an intruder when I was visiting."

"Right." Claudia's abrupt tone confused Hannah. The DI turned to PC James. "Could you get Hannah's statement typed up then she can sign it and return home?" Hannah had the distinct impression she was being fobbed off.

"Yes Guv." Hannah was amused to see the way the

younger woman looked at the DI. Like an adoring puppy.

Claudia grimaced as she tasted the coffee. "Sorry about this." She appeared tired. "Sheridan will drive you home when you've signed your statement and Hannah –" she addressed the journalist sternly – "please be careful. Don't take any risks."

Hannah didn't reply but concentrated on returning her Filofax to her bag.

"Is there anything else you haven't told us?"

"I don't think so."

The two women stared at each other. A chasm had opened between them saddening them both.

CHAPTER FORTY-ONE

Sheridan James had heard a lot about the journalist she was driving home. DI Turner was, apparently, friends with her although you wouldn't have thought so at the interview she'd just sat in on. Sheridan had been surprised both by the friendship and the differences between the two women: the cool and calculating DI and the tabloid hack who managed to expose major crimes and conspiracies but looked as though butter wouldn't melt. Even DS Benton seemed to have a high opinion of her. Although you could have cut the atmosphere with between them all with a knife when she went back in with Hannah's statement.

She'd been impressed by the safety precautions at the house when she'd collected Hannah and now waited until her passenger was safely inside before driving off.

Hannah was glad Janet was out with Elizabeth. She felt drained. She wondered about checking her emails before making the visit she dreaded but decided to get it over and done with. She reset the alarm and locked up before walking across the road to her neighbour's house.

Leah opened the door almost immediately and beamed when she saw Hannah. "Come in, come in." She turned and led her not into the kitchen where they usually sat and shared coffee and cake but into the sitting room. In contrast to Hannah's it was immaculate. Fresh flowers in vases, furniture polished, cushions plumped and neatly arranged on the sofas. A place for everything and everything in its place.

Hannah felt sick with apprehension wondering how Leah would take the news that Scott was missing. She exuded a happiness that Hannah was about to destroy.

"So what can I do for you, Hannah?" Leah smiled. "Although it's always a pleasure to see you. Do sit down."

"I reckon she'd like to join us in a glass of wine."

Hannah turned towards the door and almost forgot to breathe when she saw Scott standing there carrying a tray of nibbles, glasses and a bottle of wine. She lowered her head into her hands and a loud sob escaped her.

Leah was beside her in an instant. "Hannah whatever is the matter?" She put an arm around her shoulder.

Hannah looked up and laughed through her tears. "I came over to tell you that Scott had disappeared and..."

The young man in question handed her a glass of wine. "No way, mate. Aunty Leah invited me to stay so I was able to give up that bar job and my digs."

Hannah took a large gulp of the wine she had been handed. "Did you know your old room was broken into?"

"No I didn't. Why?"

"I don't know but I suspect it has something to do with The Child Migration Scheme."

"But that was yonks ago."

Leah had picked up her own drink, then put it down. "Is this to do with what you are working on Hannah?"

"I'm afraid so. I assume you brought all your paperwork with you Scott?"

"Sure did. And you have copies at the newspaper."

Hannah smiled. "I'm so relieved you're here."

"And so am I," Leah said. "Brian and I are planning a trip to see Adam in Australia as soon as we can and Scott's staying on for a while so we can show him some more of the UK."

"So all's well that…" Scott raised his glass to finish his sentence.

If only that were true, thought Hannah. But at least she had one less worry. "Well I'd better go. Need to let DI Turner know you're safe and sound."

"Don't go yet. Make the call from here."

Leah took her into the hall and pointed to the phone. "So wonderful to have Scott here," she whispered and kissed Hannah on the cheek.

Her call went straight through to Claudia. "Well that's a relief," she replied when Hannah explained Scott's disappearance. "But there is a connection, Hannah. It seems the person who ransacked Scott's room is the same person who attacked you and the Reverend Ian Joyce. He left another print. Either he is getting careless or thinks he's far too clever for us or knows he is immune from prosecution. However we are no nearer knowing his identity as his prints aren't on our system."

"Is he also the murderer?" Hannah could feel her skin prickling.

"That's an assumption we cannot make but it seems a distinct possibility."

Hannah took a moment to compose herself before

rejoining Scott and Leah who looked at her and asked, "Everything okay?"

"Yes. They're glad Scott isn't missing. They'll be in touch with you later."

In this sunny sitting room it was easy to imagine that all was well with the world. That there wasn't some murderer out there killing off men who'd come to find their English families.

Hannah had yet another difficult call to make when she returned home. Sheila answered more swiftly than she'd allowed for. "Oh hello Hannah. How are you?"

"Fine. I just wanted to let you know that I went to Blackwater House. There was no record of your cousin's death."

"Well we knew that." Sheila's curt tone irritated Hannah but she tried to be charitable and assume it was because she was in pain.

"Yes. And unfortunately there was a fire and all the records were destroyed."

"How convenient."

"Exactly. We don't have much else to go on. Except I'm in touch with a man in Australia who was sent over at about the same time and would have been about the same age. Is there anything else you can tell me about Derek? There's a slim possibility they knew of each other."

There was a silence at the other end of the line broken by Sheila's sudden "Of course! He walked with a limp. He was born with one of his legs shorter than the other."

"Okay. If you think of anything else let me know."

"I will. And thank you, Hannah."

Hannah replaced the receiver and felt a tremor of recognition. That limp. She paid attention to how people walked and she had an impression of something that wasn't exactly a limp. But might have been a corrected limp. She closed her eyes in an attempt to recall an image that eluded her. But nothing – or no one – came to her.

Hannah had heard from Adam Baylis via email and had arranged a time to phone him – early morning for her, evening for him. In his email Adam wrote:

"I was told my parents were dead and a new life awaited for me in the land of sunshine and oranges. It was billed as a paradise and a marvelous adventure. I know Scott has told you how I was adopted and brought up on a property in Queensland in a loving family.

"This was not the case for many of the children as, I believe, you have discovered. The physical, mental and sexual abuse many were exposed to is monstrous. I was one of the lucky ones. However I was lied to and so were my parents. That is unforgivable... what they did was evil."

Hannah dialled the number, which was answered almost immediately suggesting Adam was sitting near his phone awaiting her call.

Introductions over, Adam was effusive. "I can't say how grateful I am that you helped Scott's meet up with my sister Leah." The last two words were spoken as though his mind was still getting used to the idea of a sibling.

"I did very little, Adam. Scott has done all the legwork. He has been a real credit to you."

Adam chuckled. "He gets his brains from his mother." Hannah could hear a voice in the background. "My wife is reminding me to answer the questions in your email. Yes I have met up with some of the other child migrants. You mentioned a boy called Derek. He was not one of them. But I do remember a boy at Blackwater House of that name."

"His surname was Waterman."

"We didn't really exchange surnames. But there was something about him. He was picked on because he had a pronounced limp." Hannah sighed inwardly so far he had no information she didn't already know.

"How about the name Edward Peters? He may have been known as Eddy, Ed or Ted and was probably younger than you."

"No. Doesn't ring any bells. But I'll contact the other guys and see if they know anything."

Their conversation finished soon after Adam had thanked her again.

CHAPTER FORTY-TWO

"What on earth happened to you?" Hannah was horrified by the face in front of her. The whole of one side was lopsided and all shades of blue and black were beginning to appear under smears of blood. Her lip was cut and one eye was almost closed.

"I was mugged, wasn't I." Lucy was having difficulty pronouncing her words.

"Where? When? Have you reported it to the police?" Hannah fired her questions to alleviate her frustration and feelings of being manipulated. Why would anyone mug Lucy? She may have moved from sleeping rough to a flat but she didn't look as though she owned a bean let alone have anything of value on her.

"What's the point? They won't catch the bugger." Lucy sat gingerly in her chair. Hannah perched beside her in the hospital A&E waiting room. Edith had called her and she'd gone to St Thomas' as soon as she had been able to organise a babysitter. It had taken her a while to locate them. Although it was relatively early the waiting room was packed with people in various states of medical need. Some, she thought, would have been better off at home.

"Have you been seen by anyone?"

"The nurse took a look at me." A tear rolled down her cheek. "I was so scared I wet myself out there. She gave me a pair of paper knickers." She sniffed loudly.

Edith arrived with three coffees from the machine. "Sorry for calling you, Hannah..." She didn't finish her sentence. "I've taken some photos with my polaroid as well." She handed them to Hannah.

Hannah stared at the images. Edith had actually seen the attack. And there was one clear shot of the assailant moving away. And almost out of shot but still identifiable was someone she had definitely seen before. "Are you sure about this?"

Edith glared at her then stepped forward to push Hannah's head between her knees as she looked about to faint.

Hannah took a few deep breaths. "I know that man." She pointed to the one in the corner of the picture. "His name is Colin Helmswood – at least that's the name he gave me – and he came to see me at the newspaper offices."

"Lucy Peters?" All three women looked up. Hannah and Edith guided the patient towards the nurse. "The doctor will see you now." She made a quick assessment. "Would you like to come in on your own, Lucy?"

Lucy nodded and went with the nurse while Edith and Hannah returned to their seats.

"She's so embarrassed by her body, poor woman."

Hannah could understand that but asked the question uppermost in her mind. "How did you come to be photographing Lucy when the attack happened?"

"Pure chance. I was out and about as usual. I saw Lucy in the distance and focused in on her. Then this guy jumped her. I was too far away to stop it. The attacker fled as soon as I ran over."

"The other one too? The one I recognised?"

"No he was helping Lucy to her feet. Seemed relieved to leave her with me."

"Did he say anything?"

"Some comment about thugs and hooligans but I wasn't paying attention."

Hannah was quiet. "Have you seen him around here before?"

"No but I could check my photos to see if he has been lurking in the background." She glanced around the waiting room. "What did he see you about or is that confidential?"

"He thought he might be targeted by whoever is killing these Aussies."

Edith looked thoughtful but said nothing.

"I wonder what he was doing hanging around here?" Hannah said more to herself than in the expectation of an answer.

"Here's Lucy."

They both stood and went over to Lucy who appeared diminished by the assault. "What's the verdict?" Edith offered her an arm to lean on.

"I'll live. Nothing broken." Except her spirit thought Hannah.

Although it wasn't far back to the flats, Hannah hailed a cab. "Edith would you mind if I dropped you both off and went home?"

Lucy clasped her hand. "You get home to your little one, luv. And thanks so much for being here for me." She was still tearful and shaky.

Edith passed her the Polaroids. "I'll check through my recent contact sheets."

Hannah watched Edith take Lucy's arm as they got out of the cab and wondered why she'd thought it necessary to call her out. Maybe for moral support? Hannah sat back in the cab and closed her eyes. It seemed only minutes later that the driver pulled up outside her house.

As soon as she could the next morning Hannah phoned Claudia. Colin Helmswood had been on her mind all night. She couldn't understand what his motivation was. She had hardly slept and was exhausted wondering how he had recognised her when they first met. When Janet arrived she showed her the photos.

"Have you seen this man at all, Janet? He turned up when Lucy was assaulted last night and I'm worried about how much he seems to know about me."

Janet visibly paled. "I knew there was something strange about him."

"You've seen him hanging around here?" Hannah was appalled.

"No not here. He visited my mother."

"Sheila? Why on earth..?" Hannah thought she might know the answer to that question.

"He was there when I got home one evening. Just leaving. I was a bit earlier than usual so my mother probably thought she was safe."

"Safe?"

"Just a turn of phrase. She wouldn't say why he was there and really she doesn't have to ask my permission for anything."

"Of course not. But it might explain a few things."

Janet looked confused.

"He came to see me at the office, claiming he could be a target for whoever was killing the Australian men looking for their families. Something about him didn't add up and he had given me a false name. Right." She smiled at Janet. "I'd better ring DI Turner."

Fortunately she got straight through to Claudia and told her what had happened.

"I feel I should ring this Colin Helmswood but I'm scared. There was something about him."

"Okay." The DI was silent for a moment. Hannah felt she could almost hear her brain ticking over. "Right how about arranging to meet him somewhere safe? He came to you at *The News* offices so maybe he would again? Give him something of what you've learned to hook him. Ask him about the attack and so on. Offer him a cup of coffee so we can get some prints. And I'll have someone there to follow him when he leaves."

Hannah agreed to phone him and let Claudia know the outcome. Before calling the number she attached the recording device to the phone. Colin Helmswood gave nothing away but agreed to meet her at the newspaper offices. Hannah confirmed the arrangements with Claudia and booked an account car. She emailed her plans to Rory and left soon after.

CHAPTER FORTY-THREE

As Hannah made her way across the reception area she couldn't help but glance around to see who would be following Colin Helmswood on his departure. No one she could see. There was no time to check back with Claudia. Helmswood was walking towards her, smiling, hand outstretched.

"Hannah great to see you again. Shall I sign in?"

"Please do." Hannah smiled, safe in the knowledge that Rory would be joining them in ten minutes. He'd also set up one of the news reporters to tail their quarry when he left.

In the interview room, Hannah offered coffee. "No thank you." Her heart sank. "A glass of water would be nice, it's so hot out there."

Hannah filled a glass from the water cooler; he drank some then placed it on the table.

"So what have you discovered?"

"Well one thing is to thank you for going to the aid of a friend of mine."

"Really?" Helmswood looked mystified.

"A woman was attacked in Waterloo. You helped her."

Helmswood ran his fingers down the pleat of his chinos. "How on earth would you know about that?"

"Someone took a photograph of the attack and you appeared in the background. The photographer dashed over to help."

"Ah yes, a woman with purple hair and a strange taste

in apparel. The old lady was quite badly beaten." He stared at her. "I find it hard to imagine you two being friends. I thought she was a bag lady."

"She was. I met her through – a friend. We've kept in touch."

"Well, I didn't really do anything."

"What were you doing there?"

"I'm sorry?" His stare was so hostile it was all Hannah could do to stop herself shivering. "I wasn't aware I had to account to you for my whereabouts."

"Of course you don't. I was intrigued that's all after what you told me. The woman who was attacked – Lucy – she has a connection to Blackwater House."

Helmswood shrugged, his face a picture of polite indifference.

Hannah offered a little more. "I went there, to Blackwater House. Or at least I visited the church next to it."

Helmswood nodded. "I've been there too. All locked up now." Hannah hoped her face didn't betray what she was thinking. Was Helmswood the intruder who attacked the vicar? "Apparently there was a fire there some time ago."

"Yes – all records conveniently destroyed. What do you remember of your time there Colin?"

Helmswood stared at his manicured hands. Hannah's attention was caught by his shoes. She realised he was wearing a special shoe with an insert. To correct a limp?

"The harshness. The unbelievable cruelty of some staff."

"And the children?"

"Yes they were the worst. I was so badly beaten at one point my leg was broken. Afterwards it was never the same. My limp made them laugh at me even more."

So he wasn't Sheila's missing cousin. If he was telling the truth.

"When you came to see me before you thought you could be in danger, Colin. Have you any reason to support that now?"

"You mean because I'm still alive I'm not on a hit list?" He sounded belligerent. Rather like a child who had been caught out telling tales. "I have been taking precautions."

"I'm sure." Hannah paused. "When did you change your name?" She thought the question was worth a try.

Colin Helmswood's smile sent a shiver down her spine. "That was not one of my precautions. Now if you'll forgive me I have another appointment." He leaned forward, picked up the glass and drank the rest of the water. The empty glass slipped from his hand and shattered on the floor. "Oh I am so sorry…"

"Don't worry I'll get housekeeping to clear it. Thank you for coming in, Colin."

They walked together to reception. "Oh please sign out, sir," the receptionist called. Helmswood turned. "You do the honours, Hannah. Keep in touch." And with those parting words he was through the revolving doors and out into the sunshine. Hannah didn't bother to check if anyone was following him but went over to the reception desk.

"There you are Hannah." The receptionist handed her a clear plastic bag containing a pen. "That one was brand new and no one else except me and Mr Helmswood has touched it."

Hannah grinned. "Thanks Jackie. You're a gem."

The sound of screeching brakes, metal on metal, and a sudden explosion filled the air. Silence descended in response. Seconds passed. Jackie was already phoning the emergency services, people were running outside with extinguishers and fire blankets. Fire alarms were triggered. Hannah stood by the window watching: two cars crumpled together, ablaze. She felt a presence beside her and turned.

"Hannah, move away from the glass – just in case." Rory guided her towards the lifts.

"Do you know who those cars belong to?"

He shook his head. The pallor of his face reflected his shock. Hannah could hear the echoes of distress and disbelief around her. Security personnel were slipping seamlessly into what seemed to be well-rehearsed roles in case of terrorist attacks. Sirens could be heard outside. Paramedics, firefighters and police were swarming over the scene.

"Ms Weybridge."

Hannah turned to see a security officer walking towards her.

"I'm sorry would you mind coming with me?" His hand touched her arm.

"What for?" It was Rory who asked the question, standing steadfastly by her side.

"There seems to be a question mark over the guest you had in the interview room. He didn't sign out. Is he still in the building?"

"No he left. I was going to sign him out as…"

"Right. Could you come this way?" This time he actually grasped her arm tightly.

"Take your hand off Ms Weybridge – immediately." Rory had raised his voice so that everyone in reception could hear. He was incandescent with rage. She had always known that he fought her corner from the sidelines but this was Rory in an impressive full anger mode. Hannah noticed two other security men approaching. Their demeanour was menacing. For a second she felt faint. She prayed her legs wouldn't give way. Then the adrenaline rush took over. She would not be intimidated. She stared at the man whose expression changed from arrogant to obsequious.

"Is there a problem here?" The voice of unquestionable authority.

"No your lordship, I was just checking on Miss Weybridge's guest who hadn't signed out but apparently he has left the building."

"Good. Well I'm sure you have other duties…" Lord Gyles looked riled.

Hannah thought the three men might bow as they walked backwards into the arms of police officers waiting to arrest them. Rory had clamped his arm around her shoulders. Never had she felt so grateful to him.

"Shall we adjourn to the boardroom?" Lord Gyles smiled. "Georgina is waiting for your update."

The atmosphere in the boardroom was subdued as Hannah entered with Lord Gyles and Rory. Terry Cornhill was checking something with Georgina. Larry

Jefferson was in a corner speaking on a phone. Rory's arm guided her to a seat. He sat next to her. She could feel the support emanating from him. Unexpectedly she could smell freesias. She looked around but there were no flowers in the room.

"Okay people." Georgina commanded the attention of all in the room. "We have perhaps the most horrendous front page story for some time – right on our doorstep. Security have given the registration numbers of the cars to the police." There was a pause. "However it seems that at least three of our own security staff had been bribed – someone give Hannah a glass of water please – they are now in police custody. If it hadn't been for Lord Gyles' timely intervention we don't know what else would have happened." She paused looking round the room at each shocked face.

"Hannah – we, and the police, need all your notes, photographs etc of your dealings with Colin Helmswood. It seems he may have been in one of the cars…"

Rory gripped her hand under the table. "Do we know who was in the other?"

"Not as yet." The way Georgina replied made Hannah certain that she did know.

Larry Jefferson had apparently finished his call. "Hannah I'd just like to reassure you that your child and nanny are both safely at home and there is a police presence in the area." He made it sound so normal.

For a moment Hannah could feel everything spin. It was happening again. Another story in which she had upset someone enough to retaliate against her. And that was before her story had gone to press.

"Rory – I'd like you to interview Hannah for the news story with Larry present. But I think the police will want to go first. Hannah do you have a solicitor?"

"Yes, Neville Rogers."

"I took the liberty of phoning him for you Hannah," Larry said. "He'll be here imminently. He'll use Lord Gyles' private underground entrance as the front of the building has been sealed off."

Hannah was aware that everyone was leaving. She turned to Rory. "What terrible evil have I unleashed now?"

CHAPTER FORTY-FOUR

Hannah had been through the formal part of the police interview with DI Turner and DS Benton with PC James in attendance. Neville Rogers had arrived from his office in Chancery Lane in record time and spent a few moments alone with her. He had been well briefed by Larry Jefferson. His presence was supportive and reassuring and it was clear he had met Turner and Benton before. The questions were easily answered and Hannah handed over the pen Helmswood had used to sign in.

"That was quick thinking." Benton had actually smiled at Hannah.

"I'm learning."

DI Turner looked thoughtful. "There was no one in the first car. Apparently the driver had parked and got out for a cigarette while waiting for his passenger. He was thrown clear by the impact and suffered minor burns."

"And the second car?"

"The driver presumably activated the device to blow up the car and had time to get out. He is in custody."

"So what happened to Colin Helmswood?" Hannah was confused.

Benton and Turner exchanged a glance. "He was the passenger the first driver was waiting for." Benton paused. "Someone fitting his description was seen getting into a black cab on the main road. Looks like he was the target or set this up as some sort of elaborate hoax. "

"But why?"

"We'll need to find him to discover that."

Facts and theories were swirling in Hannah's mind. "Is there anything to link Harry Peters' death to the Australian murders?"

"What makes you ask that?"

Neville Rogers nodded. This was one aspect they had discussed earlier. Hannah took a deep breath. "There is a connection between the Peters family and Blackwater House."

"Go on." DI Turner was wearing her poker face but Hannah knew her well enough to know she wasn't going to be pleased.

"When I was going through the family papers, I found a birth certificate for a child born thirteen years after Lucy and Harry. At first Lucy denied all knowledge of a younger brother but eventually she confessed that she'd been pregnant and her mother had told her the baby had died at birth. That child ended up at Blackwater House and that's where the trail ends. He could have been sent to Australia."

"And his motive for killing his brother?"

"Revenge. Being abandoned by the family he never knew? Or it's just a coincidence?"

DI Turner shook her head. "This goes no further." Everyone in the room nodded. "Harry Peters has some sort of label stuffed into his throat. Any writing had been obliterated by the decomposition of the body. However there is nothing else – so far – to link in with the other murders."

"I don't think it's him." Hannah had everyone's attention.

"Who?"

"Colin Helmswood. I don't think he's the murderer."

"What makes you say that?"

"The photo he was caught in the night Lucy was assaulted. He is as he always looks. But the photos we have of someone stalking Harry Peters – he constantly changes his appearance. There's something else about him."

"Go on."

"I think he's some sort of priest or monk. There was the incense at Blackwater House. Reverend Ian Joyce was attacked by someone wearing a clerical collar. He said it was a good disguise near a church."

Neither DI Turner or DS Benton appeared convinced.

Sheridan James spoke for the first time. "Sarge – didn't you say there was a lingering scent in the Camberwell B&B?"

Benton shrugged his acknowledgement.

"Could it have been incense? Or some sort of holy oil they use for the last rites?" Sheridan said.

"Don't you see?" Hannah was getting into the swing of her thoughts. "This is all about religion. The institutions those young boys were taken to were run by the most despicable sadists. Maybe..." She stopped speaking. In her head she heard the words spoken to her at St John's Waterloo: *Well, well, well I wondered how long it would take you to find me here.*

"Hannah? What is it?" Claudia Turner's voice came to her as through a long tunnel.

"I've just remembered what that person said to me at St John's."

The three police officers looked at her expectantly.

"He said: 'Well, well, well I wondered how long it would take you to find me here.' Don't you see? He would gravitate to a place of worship." Hannah paused. "Plus it links in with the confidential memos I was given. And there's the ring."

"The ring?"

"The one in the photos. I managed to find someone who new about ecclesiastical rings. He had visited The Christian Brothers of the Holy Pilgrims a few years after the war. He identified the ring as being worn by those monks."

"And this priest's name?"

"The Right Reverend Joseph Mayhew. To give him his full title." Hannah gave them his telephone number.

DI Turner stood up. "Well this gets us no closer to the murderer. We have an APB out for Colin Helmswood or whoever he really is. And we need to question the security guards who were bribed to ... I wonder what they were going to do with you Hannah?" And on that awkward note the police left and Hannah was left to wonder ... and thank Neville Rogers for his help.

The front-page story the next day was a toned down version of the facts. The outrage was attributed to a terrorist attack and there was no mention of Colin Helmswood or the link to the deaths of the Australian men. A huge bouquet of flowers arrived at Hannah's home but no note to say who had sent it.

CHAPTER FORTY-FIVE

Hannah had left the answerphone to pick up calls. She wasn't in the mood to talk about what had happened. When her mobile rang, she answered. Claudia sounded harassed.

"Good you've answered. I've been ringing your landline. Are you at home?"

"Yes – is there a problem?"

"There could be. I rang your ecclesiastical ring expert."

"Yes... and..."

"He's dead." The bluntness of Claudia's announcement was an indication of her anger and frustration.

"What?" Hannah's voice was almost a screech. "When?"

"Soon after you saw him, apparently. His secretary had left for the day so he wasn't found until the next morning. Looked like a heart attack."

"But?"

"But it seems a bit too much of a coincidence, don't you think?"

The hairs on the back of Hannah's neck were almost standing to attention. She could taste her own fear in the bile which had risen in her throat. Her heart raced. Her grip on the mobile phone tightened as she swallowed hard.

"He didn't seem at all unwell when I saw him. He took a call from someone while I was there. He didn't say anything about it." Momentarily the image of the priest's face came to her. She heard the way he said evil.

Perhaps that evil had found him again. She hoped it wasn't anything to do with the fact that she'd shown him the photo of the ring. However in her heart she thought that would probably be the case.

"Hannah, I hope I don't have to tell you that you could be at risk?"

CHAPTER FORTY-SIX

"So why did my mother leave me at that place?"

If Lucy had ever considered the cardboard box she used to sleep in at the Bull Ring claustrophobic she now knew it was nothing to how she felt in her small sitting room. She was tied to one of the dining chairs. Fear made her sweat more than the heat in the room. She had opened the door to a priest who, smiling benignly, said he had some news for her. Once inside he turned into a devil, shoving a cloth into her mouth and pushing her roughly into the sitting room. It was only once she was secured to the chair and he had threatened her, that he took out the gag and asked his questions.

"Who are you?" Lucy's tears were lost on him.

"The prodigal son. Although possibly the opposite." His distain for her was matched by his arrogance. "I am your long lost brother. Although it's hard to believe we come from the same family. So I'll ask you again: why did my mother leave me at that place?"

"I didn't." The full horror of this interview was bearing down on Lucy whose voice was barely above a whisper. Her mouth was dry and the ties on her wrists and ankles dug into her flesh.

"What?" He stared into her face. "I was left at Blackwater House shortly after I was born. I was there for three years before being shipped off to Australia. Not one person cared." He spoke slowly and deliberately as he faced her, sitting on the other chair.

"I didn't know."

"Easily said." He noticed the studio portrait of her and Harry on the mantelpiece and shook his head.

"They told me the baby was born dead."

His face showed that he was slowly coming to the truth, drawing the right conclusion.

"I was thirteen." She struggled to explain herself. "I was ill and they told me the baby had died. Only recently I discovered you had survived. Hannah found your birth certificate."

"Hannah?"

"Weybridge. The journalist. She was trying to find you for me."

He drummed his fingers on the table. "Well, this isn't what I expected." His voice was calmer. Concerned.

"I know. No one would want me as a mother."

"A bit too late for mothering now, Lucy." He stood up and loomed over her.

Her eyes widened. "Please don't hurt me."

CHAPTER FORTY-SEVEN

"Lucy why didn't you tell me what had happened on the phone?" Hannah just managed to keep a lid on her anger. She'd arrived to find the door on the catch and Lucy tied to a chair in the sitting room. Apparently Edward had dialled the number for her and held the phone for Lucy to speak into. She alerted Claudia Turner as soon as she arrived; they had been so near to catching the killer.

"Why should I?" She sniffed loudly. "He had to get away. He is my son for God's sake. The baby I thought had died."

"I realise that," she said more gently, "but he may have killed your brother."

"His father." The words were spoken so quietly Hannah wasn't sure she'd heard correctly.

"I'm sorry?"

"Harry was his father." Tears were streaming down Lucy's ravaged face. "What we did was wrong but we was just kids. Twins. It just seemed natural when we did it."

Hannah placed an arm awkwardly round Lucy's shoulder. She couldn't begin to imagine what Lucy was going through. The hell of knowing that your son had killed your brother – his father – didn't bear thinking about.

"Where is he now? Do you know?"

Lucy sniffed and wiped her sleeve under her nose. "No."

"Lucy – it's not just Harry."

"What d'you mean?"

"There have been other deaths."

"Them Aussies you've been writing about?"

Hannah nodded.

Lucy sobbed. "Me mum was right then. What we did was evil and we made an evil child."

Hannah had no words to contradict her.

CHAPTER FORTY-EIGHT

Claudia Turner, Mike Benton and Hannah were sitting in the DI's office. A bottle of scotch and three empty glasses stood on the desk but as yet no one had had a drink.

"What a bloody mess." The sergeant spoke for them all but Hannah was surprised when he added, "Poor cow." He was referring to Lucy and his expression was grim. "That sort of thing used to happen more often then anyone would ever admit to. Siblings having sex and –" he shook his head and sighed.

Claudia poured them all a drink. "We have all airports and sea crossings covered. He won't get out of the country."

"Don't bet on it."

"You're being particularly defeatist, Mike. What's up?"

Mike scratched his head. "Something doesn't feel right." He glared at Hannah. "If you hadn't kept some of the facts from us…"

"Mike you can't blame a civilian for our own shortcomings." It amused Hannah to be called a "civilian" by Claudia.

For a moment Mike looked like the man she'd first met eight months ago when she'd discovered Liz Rayman's dead body in the crypt at St John the Evangelist at Waterloo – gumpy and unkind – not the man she'd come to respect and have reason to be thankful to.

"I know, I know – it's just so frustrating. Especially after your great work Hannah." He smiled at her.

"Well that's a first." Claudia topped up their glasses.

"What's a first?"

Three faces turned towards the figure in the doorway looking slightly tired but relaxed.

"Where the hell have you been?" It was Claudia who spoke first.

"Australia, mate." Tom Jordan grinned.

Hannah could have killed him. Why hadn't he let her know? Warned her that he'd be turning up like this? A hundred emotions swirled within her.

Mike Benton went off for another chair and a glass as Tom slipped the rucksack he had slung on one shoulder to the floor. He kissed Hannah briefly, smiling all the time as he hugged Claudia and then sat down. Mike returned.

"I'm sorry to spring this on you. I was sent out to investigate someone." He looked directly at Hannah. "You saw some redacted papers –"

"How do you know about that?" Her voice was icy in contrast to the heat in the room.

"Let's just say I heard you had been contacted."

Claudia poured Tom a drink. "Right let's cut to the chase shall we? We assume that you were sent out to discover something – anything – about this Christian Brotherhood of the Holy Pilgrims that's supposed to have disappeared off the face of the earth after a fire."

Benton leaned back in his chair alert to his boss's tone and obviously enjoying her barely contained fury aimed at Tom.

"How long have you been back?" Hannah's voice cut the air.

Tom smiled at her. "I called in at your home before coming here. After I had been to the ministry. I was told to liaise with you, Claudia." He took a large gulp from his drink. "I found the erstwhile head of the Brotherhood living quietly and seemingly anonymously in Brisbane. He's very old now but has been directing a clean up operation both in Australia and, as you have discovered, in the UK, using a monk who has lived with him since the fire – and before. I can't go into details. The Aussies have clamped down. But I think –"

There was a knock on the door and Sheridan James entered. "Excuse me ma'am but we have a positive ID for Colin Helmswood from the fingerprint Hannah managed to get." She saw Tom and stopped.

"Well don't keep us in suspense." Claudia smiled at her.

"His name is Colin Holton and that's not all. He's been detained at Heathrow."

Claudia was already on her feet. "We'll take two cars – I'm assuming you'd like to come along for the ride Hannah? Sheridan you can drive me. Hannah with Mike."

"Yes ma'am." She was grinning.

Tom also stood up. "Right I need to get back." He didn't explain why. "See you all later." His smile encompassed them all and Hannah could quite cheerfully have slapped it from his face.

They arrived in Heathrow in record time. Hannah had phoned Rory whilst en route and he had found a photographer who was already at the airport for some celebrity departure. He gave Hannah his mobile number so they could liaise. Claudia had given them a precise area to meet and the photographer was there along with Sheridan James and the DI who had arrived slightly ahead of them.

Hannah could see Claudia was speaking into her radio. She had radioed Mike to say that Colin Holton had been detained by airport security. As they made their way across the concourse, Hannah noticed a man staring at her. A priest. There was something familiar about him. As they drew nearer, he picked up the suitcase at his side. She noticed his ring. From that distance she couldn't see it properly but... She turned to Mike and embraced him.

"That's him –" her voice a whisper in his ear. "The priest. I'm sure it's him." He moved to see.

"Play along." He took her hand and walked towards their target only a metre or two away just as he walked in their direction. He bumped Hannah's shoulder and she felt a sharp pain in her side. Benton pounced and had the priest on the floor and cuffed as Hannah slid to the ground.

CHAPTER FORTY-NINE

Colin Holten wouldn't stop talking. Now that he had been apprehended he wanted the world to know what he'd been up to trying to expose the abuse that The Christian Brotherhood of the Holy Pilgrims had inflicted on the boys in their care.

"Where's Hannah Weybridge? She should hear this."

"All in good time Mr Holten." DI Turner had watched in horror as Hannah collapsed to the floor, fervently hoping that the wound was less serious than it appeared from the amount of blood she was losing. She had sent Sheridan with her in the ambulance.

The priest was escorted away by armed officers while she and Mike arranged for him to be taken back into central London.

"So Mr Holton, you have been detained by airport security under the Prevention of Terrorism Act. I am here to inform you that –" She paused as the door opened, a look of disbelief on her face as Tom Jordan strode in with two officers by his side.

"DI Turner I have a Warrant here for the arrest of Colin Holton. Mr Holton you are charged with –"

DS Benton stood. Jordan shook his head and handed over the warrant to Claudia who glanced at it then turned to her sergeant. "Come on we have other fish to fry." And without another word, they left the room closing the door silently behind them.

"Do you think he knows what's happened to Hannah?"

Benton was struggling to make sense of what had just happened.

"I have no idea. Let's focus on Edward Peters." And with that they parted to drive back in the separate cars they had arrived in.

Hannah came to on a stretcher in the ambulance with Sheridan James by her side. She tried to remove the oxygen mask on her face.

"Don't try to talk, Hannah. Everything's going to be okay." Sheridan smiled but she felt like crying.

"Elizabeth." The word escaped her like a sigh as the paramedic shoved Sheridan out of the way.

CHAPTER FIFTY

DI Turner stood before the custody sergeant. "Would you mind repeating that?"

"I'm sorry ma'am. The prisoner Edward Peters was dead on arrival. He was transferred to the mortuary at Kings awaiting a post mortem. The attending pathologist said it –" he referred to the sheet of paper – "appeared he'd taken some sort of suicide pill."

Claudia looked as though she had a great deal more to say but Benton who had been taking a call on his mobile, touched her arm. "Hannah's undergoing surgery right now."

"Where are Edwards' possessions? Presumably he was searched? They obviously missed the suicide pill but what about the weapon he used on his victim?"

"There was no weapon ma'am," the duty sergeant replied.

If Claudia had had any weapon to hand, Benton thought she would use it then and there. "So how did he manage to stab Ms Weybridge?"

"It was his crucifix, guv." Benton shuddered as he remembered the scene. "There was a blade hidden in it like a flick knife."

CHAPTER FIFTY-ONE

Hannah was sitting propped up by pillows. The hospital bed wasn't comfortable and nor was the look James was giving her as he held the hand that wasn't connected to the drip. She tried to smile.

"What am I going to do with you?" He stroked her hand and his eyes were suspiciously wet. "I couldn't believe it when I saw your name on the emergency list." He coughed. "You are so lucky. Your assailant managed to miss all your vital organs and pierced a muscle. Hence all the blood loss."

Hannah smiled. "Thank you."

"Janet contacted your parents and they are with Elizabeth."

"That was quick."

"They were flown over by Lord Gyles."

Hannah digested this. Someone had brought in all the newspapers and she had been front-page news. The photographer had got a lot more than he'd expected. She knew there was a police guard outside her hospital room.

"When can I go home?"

"Not my call." James bleep sounded and he sighed. "Don't get up to mischief while I'm gone." He kissed her on the forehead and left the room.

She must have dozed and when she woke again Tom was sitting in a chair by her bed. He was the last person she wanted to see.

"How are you feeling?"

Hannah sighed then groaned as she tried to sit up. Tom was immediately by her side, arranging her pillows and passing her a cup with a straw.

"Thanks."

He smiled but his eyes looked tired and wary. "I'm so sorry I couldn't let you know what I was doing. Where I was. I –"

"Tom I don't want to talk at the moment. I want to get out of here and I want to see my daughter." Her eyes filled with tears. "There was a moment when I thought I was going to die and she would be…" she sniffed. "I need some time."

Tom took that as his cue to leave and she sank back onto the pillows and wept.

EPILOGUE
Two weeks later

Hannah picked up the photocopy of Edward Peters' notebook that Claudia had given her to read. She and Mike Benton had filled her in on Colin Holten's attempts to expose the horrific abuse perpetrated by The Christian Brotherhood of the Holy Pilgrims – or what was left of them. The head of the organisation, whom Tom had tracked down, had been arrested in Brisbane. Tom was now back there with Holten. Hannah was glad she didn't have to face questions about their future – if any – together. Edward Peters was dead. She wondered how Lucy was feeling. Devastated she supposed.

And here were Edward Peters' thoughts. Sitting on a sun lounger in her parents' garden in France – so far away from what had happened in London – Hannah hesitated to open it. Did she really want to know what had gone on in his mind? A priest who wore a crucifix harbouring a flick-knife? A man who as a baby had been rejected and, as a child had had his mind infected by a terrible evil? She sighed. She had been left with a visible scar – his had been concealed but ran much deeper she feared.

She opened the notebook and flicked through the pages. Her eyes were drawn to a name written in capitals and underlined: HARRY PETERS.

It had been easier than I'd imagined to trace him even though he wasn't on my official list. I'd spent so much of my life wondering what it would feel like coming face to face with my quarry. All those years of picturing faces. Imagining features. Fantasising about reactions. Recognition. Would my skin tingle in acknowledgement? Now I knew. Nothing. Nothing inside me responded, corresponded and I had stalked him for some days. I'd even bought him a drink in the pub he frequented.

"Do you know who I am?" I asked him after I had slipped into his flat.

The man muttered something I couldn't understand. I pulled his chin so that he faced me. "Do you know who I am?" The old man's eyes widened in fear as I pushed the capsule into his mouth and passed his drink so he would swallow it.

He dribbled onto my hand. Fortunately, I was wearing latex gloves. His lack of dignity disgusted me. Then I noticed that he had pissed himself. What an abject specimen of humanity.

It was dark outside but the overhead light was on casting a strange quality of light and shadow. I am beyond compassion now for this brother who denied my existence. This family who rejected me. The cyanide was taking effect. His mouth dropped open. Into it I thrust the label I had carried with me for all those years. The label I wore when I was sent to the land of sunshine and oranges. I was lucky that the Brothers adopted me, brought me up to become one of them rather than abuse me as they had the others. The fact that I was so young saved me. Now I was in London to repay my debt. But this was personal.

I turned off the television sets and the overhead light

in the sitting room. The hall light remained on as I slipped out of the door and out of his death. I felt a charge of adrenaline. As I left the square I pulled off the gloves and my hat and dumped them in a bin. I ran my fingers through my hair and smiled at patrons leaving the Old Vic theatre. The evening was warm so I walked over Waterloo Bridge – a part of a landscape that had rejected me. I have made my mark. Created memories that people will wish they didn't have. Left my presence. My mission will fan out like ripples in a pond. From one side of the world to the other. No one's world will be the same. Mine included. But I am strong. This is what I was brought up to do. My whole life has been leading me to this point.

Hannah skimmed on not wishing to absorb the evil within the pages. Then a date caught her eye: Monday 27 June, 1994 – the day Lucy had found the dead body of her brother.

I watched her climbing the steps, slowly. She paused often as though out of breath. It was hot and she was not dressed for the heat. I had no interest in her until she reached the fourth floor and number 39. No one – as far as I was aware – had been there since my visit. So disappointing to have my deed ignored.

But back to the woman. A bag lady! Who'd have thought she would be the one to discover my work. Her and that weird next-door neighbour. Who is she? She had a key! I watched as she rushed out and I slipped away as the sirens grew louder and the police arrived.

She flicked further on and saw another name she recognised: Jeff Collins.

I love London. I didn't think I would but it suits me and my purposes. It's teeming with tourists. I am one among so many. Nobody knows I'm here. My anonymity makes me invisible and yet I can be seen. I am connected by a thin thread, which may snap at any moment.

I used to feel I was just marking time. All those years I was a sleeper for so long. A sleeper who had left no footprint. But I have now. There's no mistaking my work. Take Jeff Collins. Couldn't entice him out of that bloody library. A challenge but not impossible.

I will be acknowledged. And when I return home I shall reap the rewards.

Hannah paused and sipped some water. The arrogant tone of Edwards writing was abhorrent to her. She flicked through a few more pages.

Manchester didn't suit me. Fortunately my mark was easily found and disposed of and I could return to London for my final victim. I am getting to know this city well. My talent for camouflage has stood me in good stead. I blend in. I am non-descript. But this is not the character I see in the mirror. My reflection shows strength and determination.

For security I have changed hotels three times. Finance has been no object so currently I am at the Strand Palace. I should have preferred the Savoy with a river view but I fear I would draw more attention there.

I am looking forward to leaving the UK.

The newspapers have gradually picked up on my work. That journalist Hannah Weybridge on The News *has a lot to answer for. I am tempted to teach her a lesson but fear it would get too personal especially as she is connected to someone else I must see before I leave.*

Spring will soon arrive at home and I am looking forward to a retreat. I feel drained by my mission. Especially now. Retribution is a divine sensation. I have been royally entertained but I feel the need to recoup my strength. Recharge my batteries.

Seeing her own name made Hannah's stomach clench. Then she saw the entry for his last victim in Camberwell.

It must be high on the list of circumstances that could haunt you as you get older. The thought of having a heart attack when you are on your own and with no hope or means of contacting anyone.

Even worse, I imagine, would be having someone like me sitting next to you waiting for your last gasp. Someone unknown, staring at you as though you were a scientific specimen. No empathy. No compassion. But also no judgement.

I do not judge. I don't care if you weep or swear. Dribble or fart. Wet yourself. It's all the same to me. I have seen it all before. Nothing shocks me. Sickens me. I see the fear and I absolve you. Silently. I say nothing. I wait with you until it is over. Only you know why I am here. Too late. No one else makes any connection. I love the look of realisation at the end and I slip away and leave you. Our association dissolves.

You, my friend, are taking longer than the others. Your eyes stare at me in horror. Fear. You open your mouth but no words emerge, just gargling sounds. You are drowning in your own spit. Interesting contortions of your facial features.

It's hot. But not so hot as where you'll be going. I smile at my little unspoken joke. The last breath is released from your body. My job is done.

And so was hers. Hannah wept for Edward, the abandoned baby, yet she felt nothing but relief in his death. She heard the patio doors open and closed the notebook. The rest of its contents could wait. Hannah opened her arms to the one person who could dispel her gloom who made life complete. Elizabeth. She clasped her close and breathed in her fragrance.

Elizabeth twisted in her arms. She stared into her mother's eyes. "Love you, Mama."

"Love you too." It felt as though there was no room in her heart for anyone else.

ACKNOWLEDGEMENTS

No book is written in isolation – at least not mine. I am blessed with having friends who act as cheerleaders, buck me up and keep me focused and I am indebted to them. For fear of forgetting someone, no names but you know who you are.

My gratitude as always to Matthew Smith and the team at Urbane Publications who still believe in Hannah Weybridge and her journey to book four.

A huge thank you to Lorna Byrne and Saša Janovic who gave valuable feedback from reading the earlier drafts of Perdition's Child and to Elizabeth Stanton who picked up a historical error and Charlotte Oram who bowled me over with her enthusiasm.

Sheridan James will see herself in a new light having mentioned to me that being a character in a book was on her bucket list. So from vicar to police officer with one wave of my writer's wand. Hope she likes her new persona!

As ever any mistakes in the narrative are my own but I checked the Australian dialogue with Kylie Bryant, some medical facts with Geoff Lockwood and Ian Patrick gave me some guidance on policing in the Met in the 1990s.

Simpsons in the Strand is a fascinating building with a unique history that was shared with me by the restaurant manager Roy White when Harriet and I enjoyed a delicious lunch there. And a big thank you to Harriet who is my mini PR telling everyone her mémé is an author, and reels off titles of my books. The loving encouragement from her and my fabulous daughter, Olivia keeps me going during dark days.

I am humbled by the generosity of authors and book bloggers whose support I have enjoyed and of course a huge thank you to readers who kindly leave reviews and let me know how much they have enjoyed meeting Hannah Weybridge. I hope you all enjoy the next installment in her career.

For most of her working life in publishing, Anne has had a foot in both camps as a writer and an editor, moving from book publishing to magazines and then freelancing in both. Having edited both fiction and narrative non-fiction, Anne has also had short stories published in a variety of magazines including *Bella* and *Candis* and is the author of seven non-fiction books. Telling stories is Anne's first love and nearly all her short fiction as well as the Hannah Weybridge series began with a real event followed by a 'what if …'; That is also the case with the two prize-winning 99Fiction.net stories: *Codewords* and *Eternal Love*. *Perdition's Child* is her fourth thriller starring investigative journalist Hannah Weybridge.

HAVE YOU DISCOVERED THE OTHER HANNAH WEYBRIDGE THRILLERS?

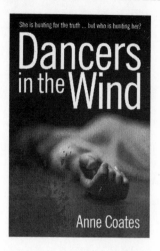

She is hunting for the truth, but who is hunting her?

Freelance journalist and single mother Hannah Weybridge is commissioned by a national newspaper to write an investigative article on the notorious red light district in Kings Cross. There she meets prostitute Princess, and police inspector in the vice squad, Tom Jordan. When Princess later arrives on her doorstep beaten up so badly she is barely recognisable, Hannah has to make some tough decisions and is drawn ever deeper into the world of deceit and violence.

Three sex workers are murdered, their deaths covered up in a media blackout, and Hannah herself is under threat. As she comes to realise that the taste for vice reaches into the higher echelons of the great and the good, Hannah understands she must do everything in her power to expose the truth .... and stay alive.

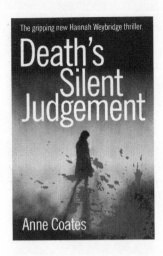

The gripping new Hannah Weybridge thriller.

Death's Silent Judgement

Anne Coates

DEATH'S SILENT JUDGEMENT is the thrilling sequel to *Dancers in the Wind* and continues the gripping series starring London-based investigative journalist Hannah Weybridge.

Following the deadly events of *Dancers in the Wind*, freelance journalist and single mother Hannah Weybridge is thrown into the heart of a horrific murder investigation when a friend, Liz Rayman, is found with her throat slashed at her dental practice.

With few clues to the apparently motiveless crime Hannah throws herself into discovering the reason for her friend's brutal murder and is determined to unmask the killer. But before long Hannah's investigations place her in mortal danger, her hunt for the truth placing her in the path of a remorseless killer...

The series is very much in the best traditions of British women crime writers such as Lynda La Plante and Martina Cole.

'Gripping and original, the most thrilling Hannah Weybridge investigation yet.' HUGH FRASER

Songs of Innocence

Anne Coates

"Gripping and original, Anne Coates delivers the most thrilling Hannah Weybridge investigation yet."
– Hugh Fraser, bestselling author of the Rina Walker thriller series

A woman's body is found in a lake. Is it a sad case of suicide or something more sinister? Hannah Weybridge, still reeling from her friend's horrific murder and the attempts on her own life, doesn't want to get involved, but reluctantly agrees to look into the matter for the family.

The past however still stalks her steps, and a hidden danger accompanies her every move.

The third in the bestselling Hannah Weybridge thriller series, *Songs of Innocence* provides Hannah with her toughest and deadliest assignment yet...

Urbane

PUBLICATIONS

Urbane Publications is dedicated to
developing books that challenge,
thrills and fascinate.

From page-turning thrillers to
ground-breaking non-fiction, our goal is to
publish what YOU want to read.

Find out more at
urbanepublications.com